Goodnight My Bleeding

Rose

D. S. Gore

First Paperbacks edition September 2017

Copyright © 2017 by D. S. Gore

Designed by Anna Orlova

Edited by Sutton Mason

ISBN - 13: 978-0692945438

Printed in the United States of America

Goodnight My

Bleeding Rose

1

After all that's happened, I think I finally have the time to sit down, take this God-forsaken bullet out of my head, and tell you a little bit about my never-ending hike from birth to hell—basically all of it.

I'll be speaking differently than I am now, almost as if I'm a refined person, if that makes sense to any of you… Not only that, but I'll be dressed differently. I'll act differently and look at others differently. Strangely enough, I'll be the opposite of my current self. That's because everything seems different when you're a ghost. For one thing, you could be an extroverted genius while you're alive and breathing, and yet the second your body takes on the form of an invisible cloud, *boom*—you're a nobody. Your confidence plummets into the depths of the Earth like a meteor falling from outer space, quickly breaking apart as the humans on the surface run away and scream for their lives. Your eyes lose their once unique color, and your vigor turns into a void of procrastination. As time moves forward, your emotions disappear. Everything seems to happen faster than the blink of an eye, all while the living mourn for you. I find it all so strange. After all, who wouldn't?

Anyway, I'll stop wasting your time and get right into telling you everything.

Our truck came to a stop. The back doors suddenly flew open and a bunch of soldiers in army-like uniforms rushed inside. One of the men grabbed my right arm and pushed me out of the back, yelling something that I couldn't make out at the time. Before I could even look up, another two men hastily grabbed my shoulders and dragged me forward.

"Hey! Let go of me! Let go, goddammit!" I yelled, bewildered by everything that was going on.

"Shut up!" A guard yelled.

"What are you doing? Let me go!"

In response to my plea, the guards threw me into a giant, crowded room, along with everyone else who was crammed into the back of that tarnished truck with me.

Even though my state of panic continued to linger, I got up and looked around. The building surrounding me was large enough to start an epidemic. Over five hundred people were packed inside while another few hundred were still being pushed through the steel gates.

What is this place? I thought to myself.

What have I done? Is this all a punishment? Everything seems so foggy to me, and I can't seem to understand why... I know I'm alive; everything feels too real for me to be dead.

The room had a very basic layout. To my left, there was a giant gray door glaring over a large crowd of children and their anxious, teary-eyed parents. And to my right, there was a set of train rails which passed through the center of the room, separating one side from the other. That was all; everything was as bland as it could be.

In a desperate attempt to find out where I was, I trudged through the crowd of living confusion. Eventually, I stumbled upon a small group of people; they were all staring at a sign which was embedded into the wall. It stated:

This room is designated for the caves. One hundred of the prisoners here will have the advantage of entering the train while everyone else will be executed. Best of luck to the souls who fulfill their desires. Sincerely,

President Marcus

As reality tried to set in, I thought to myself, *What the hell did I just read?*

That was when a set of speakers behind the train rails activated. A loud noise suddenly pierced my ears from the PA system, along with everybody else's. A guard stepped onto a small wooden podium and waited until the room calmed down. When everyone in the crowd grew quiet, the guard took a pin from his pocket and dropped it to the floor. Everyone in the room could hear the pin vibrate as it hit the ground.

He cleared his throat and began to speak.

"I know everyone in this room is confused, so I'll read a speech given to me by the coordinator of this prison to calm all of you down."

Parts of the room began to murmur louder than the others. But when one of the head guards yelled "Quiet!" the sounds of confused murmuring quickly vanished. The guard standing on the podium took a tattered piece of paper from his pocket, along with a pair of small reading glasses, and placed them where they belonged. During this time, I noticed that all the guards were wearing the same uniform: camouflage blue suits with a wall of scarlet stars printed on the sleeves, old black shoes, and mud-ridden caps that looked dirtier than the floor beneath us.

As the room turned silent again, the guard continued to read: "Anyone standing inside this room today has their own reasons for why they are here. But for the most part, you were sent here because you committed a crime. If not, then the authorities think of you as a disruption to regular life."

The guard paused to clear his throat again, and then continued, "Now, since you understand why you're here, we can move on to the main event. In a few minutes, a large train will appear in front of you. If you do not make it on, then you will be executed."

At that very moment, the room erupted into pandemonium. I could hear a frenzy of endless crying, people screaming swear words more than anything else, and an unsettling violence lurking all around me, slowly pulling me in like a merciless tornado. Without having much time to think, I pushed through several crowds of people who were all very upset, trying to hide from the guards while also rushing towards the train rails. I wasn't sure what to do. Everything was moving so quickly.

As I pushed my way into the center of the crowd, I heard a loud noise come from a short distance away; it was time. A giant train flew from a dark tunnel into the room. Multiple doors opened and people started to flood inside while the guards were keeping an eye on anyone who entered.

I whispered to myself, "What's going on? Do I... Do I try to run away?"

Eventually, I decided to follow the crowd, but as I rushed toward the train, I looked to my left and saw a tall, skinny man suddenly stop when one of the guards grabbed a little child by his shoulder. I wasn't sure if the child was his son or not, but those kinds of details didn't really seem to matter at the time. Without hesitating, the skinny man punched the guard with full force. The guard dropped to the floor while the child fell on the ground crying.

I heard him ask, "Are you alright?"

He nodded, so the skinny man smiled and helped the kid stand back up. But as fate would have it, another guard ran up to the skinny man and pointed a pistol up between his eyes.

"No, don't hurt my dad!" the little child screamed.

He tried to run in between his father and the guard, but his father held him back.

The guard yelled, "Go away, before I kill you too you brat!"

As the man closed his eyes and grasped his son in his arms, the guard pulled the trigger and watched the skinny man fall to his knees.

"Dad?" The kid's eyes teared up. "Dad? Talk to me!"

A pool of blood emerged from the back of his father's head, slowly consuming the ground beneath them.

"Please... Dad..."

With his hands now showered in his own father's blood, the kid started to scream, so the guard reloaded his weapon and shot him straight between the eyes as well. For a moment, I stopped and stared at the guard. I could feel a tempest of fear and bewilderment slowly growing inside of me.

"What the hell is this place?" I whispered to myself, now shivering more than ever. "Where am I?"

The sounds of gunfire suddenly became ubiquitous. The people who had some sort of intelligence entered the train while the others spent the end of their lives getting gunned down. All I could see was pure chaos; that and the screams of hundreds of desperate prisoners now taking over the room.

As the train grew fuller and fuller by the minute, the loudspeakers exclaimed, "This is your last chance to board."

Where am I supposed to go? Where are these men taking us? This is all too much! I thought. *Am I awake? Is this all truly real?*

The train doors were starting to close. Hundreds of people were still attempting to board, now with greater ferocity.

"Wait!" I yelled, struggling through the crowd. "Wait for me! Please!"

I tried running towards the train, but somebody from the crowd grasped my shoulder and mumbled, "Sorry bud, but you're too late."

"No… The doors are still closing. We still have time!"

But as it turned out, the train doors were already shut. That was when I heard a loud boom ravage through the air behind me. It was a group of guards, pulling the triggers on their guns and wiping out the first line of prisoners by the train. They were synchronized when they fired, almost as if they'd trained for this moment for over a decade.

What did I do to deserve this? I thought. *What is all of this?*

The levels of blood were starting to rise like a flash flood as the train slowly took off. The room was now congested with guards and bloodshed, defending the outside world from the prisoners all around me. Some tried to run away while others ran at the guards, hoping to stampede them in a last-ditch effort to escape with their lives.

I kneeled behind a pile of bodies bordering the train tracks and said to myself, "What do I do?"

Boom.

With greater panic in my voice, I continued, "Dammit, what do I do?"

The next *boom* was followed by a chorus of screams.

Without thinking, I started to run toward the train; a desperate idea had popped into my head. I attempted to avoid the lifeless bodies bordering the railway but avoiding them was almost impossible since the floor itself had turned redder than a rose. Nonetheless, I made it to the tracks. The train started to pass a gateway which led out of the room, and I knew that it was going to close soon. With the little time I had left, I chased after the train, but as I reached the threshold of the gate, a group of guards quickly spotted me and pointed multiple rifles at my forehead. I continued to run after the train along the tracks, thinking I could have so many more deserved opportunities in what seemed like a transient life. This wasn't my time to die. At least, not yet.

The guards took their shots and missed, hitting the metal door which was slowly closing at the end of the track. Without having anything left to lose, I jumped onto the back of the train, grabbing a slim metal bar which was about a foot from the ground. The next thing I could feel were my scrawny legs sliding against a pathway of dirt, rock, and wood while the light around me grew dimmer and dimmer by the second.

After the train turned a corner, my arm gave up—I let go of the bar and fell, feeling an endless wave of stones ravage whatever was left of my legs. I got up with a cascade of endless pain flowing through my nerves. But I knew I couldn't sit in one spot and wait for something to happen, so I picked myself up and dragged my feet across the jagged gravel floor. While I struggled to follow the lights against the walls, everything seemed to grow darker. Were my eyes getting tired? Was I getting a migraine from the same few questions that kept repeating in my head?

Where am I?

Why were they trying to kill me?

What did I do?

Why am I here?

How did I get out of that mess alive?

I was inside a giant cage of confusion and darkness. For some strange reason, I felt like death was always watching me, waiting for me to make a mistake.

An hour had passed. I spent that time dragging my feet along the train rails, hoping that I would soon reach a light source, if there even was one at the end of the tunnel.

Eventually, I turned a corner, which was strange because I had been walking in a straight line ever since my arm let go of the train. As I reached the end of the track, a giant burst of light suddenly blinded me. When I reopened my eyes, I saw a circle of torches on totem poles sticking out of the ground, and the thousands of people walking through a series of caves behind them.

I walked into the brightness, even though I was still hesitant about everything around me. The light didn't feel natural—nothing did; in a way, everything about this place felt somewhat gloomy. I didn't see any grass, nor did I see anything green; everything was a mix of red and black, the colors of calamity. As I continued looking around me, I found myself standing next to one of the totem poles. There were red symbols on it that looked almost satanic. I touched one, feeling the wood; it felt somewhat rubbery. It wasn't natural and for some reason I felt disappointed.

Could the fire be fake as well?

The fire felt real to me. I could feel the pain in my skin as I walked closer to it, which relieved me of something: I wasn't dreaming, and I surely wasn't dead.

I wanted to get closer; I wanted to touch the flames. But that was when I felt a hand slither onto my shoulder; it was warmer than any hand I'd ever felt before.

After a moment of brief and awkward silence, I looked to my left and found a group of seemingly frightened children staring at me. I touched my shoulder because I wasn't sure if something was truly there or not, but as it turned out, something was definitely there. The children took a step back and the person who was touching my shoulder turned me around, transforming my emotions into stone.

2

I froze up, waiting to see the first living soul who would discover me in this stone-showered prison. As I turned around, a short long-haired woman stood there, staring at me; she was skeptical of something.

"Hello?" I muttered.

I looked back at the crowd of children who were now sitting on the floor behind her. As I continued to look around, I found that certain parts of the cave were only somewhat dark while others were pitch black, so I guess the children considered this particular spot to be well lit.

In an apprehensive voice, the woman said, "Hello?"

She was wearing a fluorescent pink dress that grazed her grimy knees. I stepped back as a sign for the woman to take her hand off my shoulder and, in an awkward voice, replied, "Do you want something from me?"

"Why are you on school grounds?"

I looked around some more and saw a schoolhouse in the distance.

Who in their right mind would want to put a school here?

"Oh, sorry… I don't really know where I am. Who are you?"

"They call me Miss Annabelle."

"Who's 'they'?" I asked.

"Who do you think? Actually, that shouldn't matter right now… Don't you have friends around these parts of the caves that you should be spending your time with right now?"

She sounded annoyed.

"Uhm… No, I guess not."

In a now surprised voice, she said, "What? You don't have any friends down here?"

What? Why do you care if I have friends or not?

"No," I replied. "Why is that an issue?"

She ignored my question and took a step closer. "What? You know it's dangerous to be alone down here, right?"

"Why would not having friends be dangerous?"

After Miss Annabelle processed the stupidity of my question, she took a step back and repeated, "Really? You don't have any friends down here? Not one?"

"Are you deaf or something? I said no."

Miss Annabelle stroked her hair and started to think some more. I couldn't believe that such a simple, yet random conversation needed to be thought about.

"Are you okay?" I continued. "You look like you're about to faint."

Just then, she grew nervous. I could tell because her voice shook when she whispered, "You must be an Atara." Clearly, she didn't want the children to hear her.

"Huh? What are you going on about?" I replied.

"Why are you here?" She said, now terrified.

"Are you crazy or something?"

She ignored my last remark and continued, "No, no, you should be with the other Atara."

Seriously, what the hell is this woman going on about?

"What's that? An Atara?"

She took another step back and continued, "Atara are the new prisoners who arrive here. You can't be here yet—it's too early for you to go wandering off already."

"Alright… Then where am I supposed to go?"

"You should be at the station with the others. Hurry, or they'll lock you up," she urged.

"But this is a prison, isn't it? I'm already locked up."

Miss Annabelle turned away and ordered the children to get up and run back to the schoolhouse. As she watched them hurry off, I noticed a small stamp that was on her hand. It was red and the symbols in its design were the same ones I'd noticed on the totem poles from earlier.

After parting ways with that strange woman, I found myself on top of a steep, stone hill which bordered an even smaller building made of wood. I looked into the distance and saw a crossroad of pathways which led into a series of smaller caves. Thousands of prisoners, along with animals like dogs and donkeys, were walking into the abyss. I assumed the farmers brought along animals like donkeys down here for work reasons because in my mind, it made no sense to keep one as a pet when you're living in a rock.

Anyway, after watching the crowd move along for a little while, I decided to ask for directions, so I made my way down the hill, hoping to nourish my growing curiosity, and tapped on a passerby's shoulder.

I asked him, "Sorry, but could you tell me the name of this road?"

The man mumbled, "No idea" and kept walking.

"Wait!" I exclaimed. "Can you at least tell me where I can find a map or something?"

He ignored me.

Since I was desperate, I figured that if I followed him, the chances my questions being answered could only rise. So, I followed the stranger. The man was wearing an old leather jacket and a pair of gray jeans. He was also wearing a dirty silver-colored hat, different from what the guards were wearing, but it seemed similar.

An hour later, I lost sight of the stranger and ended up in some sort of plaza which had hundreds of "houses" that were built into the walls, except for one. There was a giant quartz building in the center of everything that overlooked all the others. The structure was enormous, and the other prisoners were unable to enter. The front entrance was guarded by two brawny men, and the door itself was taller than any other door I'd ever seen before.

As I moved closer to the front of the building, I saw a giant group of people, cheering and screaming until their voices turned to dust. I wasn't sure what was being discussed, so I turned away and kept walking. That was when a group of muscular men approached me from out of nowhere, quickly pushing me to the floor.

"Hey, what are you doing?" I yelled, with my knees now forced into the ground.

"Stop!" I yelled. "Help! Someone! Help me!"

Everything suddenly grew dark. The man in front of me, whom I had followed earlier, came out from the crowd, and hit me over the head with a battered wooden stick.

I stopped thinking.

Everything turned black and I was taken away from the blood light.

* * *

What am I doing here? I thought. *Is it because of my family? Dad's government job? Was I framed?*

Is it my fault that I'm stuck down here?

Is it because I rebelled? No… Dad wouldn't do this to me.

At some point in my childhood, my dad changed; he was offered a bigger position in the government. At least, that was all I was ever told.

A few months after his promotion, we moved into a great new home overlooking the city, but I was never told why we'd moved or where I was in the world.

From then on, when I got up to go to school every morning, my father had a guard escort me. I was ordered to take the same route every day and, on the weekends, I was like a bar of gold inside a vault, stuck in the house from Saturday morning to Sunday night. After the tenth grade, I was able to memorize every landmark on that single pathway. Each tree, every strand of grass, house, rock, whatever. That was the same case within my home; that was where I spent most of my time.

By the end of high school, life seemed dull. I saw my father once or twice a month and all he ever said to me was, "Are you listening to your mother?" That was it.

My answer to that question every time was, "Yes, yes I am." And after that, he'd just nod and walk away. I always wished I would've said, "no," just to see what would've happened.

When I turned eighteen and started my first year at university, I felt like I lost all my privacy, along with my sanity. The guard who had followed me to school every day was now my roommate. I wasn't allowed to talk to anyone; I was only permitted to talk with my professors and the guard. I felt constricted and there was nothing I could do about it. My father was powerful, and I was the weakling.

Just after university, I was transferred back home where my dad was standing at the entrance to the house. He was holding a small black box which looked like the definition of despair. It was so dreadful because it was all stained and scratched up; my father had never given me anything like that before. Eventually, he told me that my mother had died from "unknown circumstances", and he gave me the box. I opened it to find my mother's favorite necklace sitting inside. I was upset, which was not a foreign feeling to me because I had experienced sadness every single day in my seemingly endless life of isolation.

After my mother's death, my father made me move once again—I don't remember where he wanted to send me. All I remember is that I refused to go. I was tired of living under him.

"You can't control my life!" I screamed. "Leave me alone!"

"Get away from me! You're ruining my life! Get away!"

And that's the last thing I remember before being knocked out and sent into the truck that brought me into these caves.

There's no way that my dad would try to kill me... He wouldn't keep me down here either.

There's just no way a father would do that to his son...

_3_

I woke up from a deep unintentional sleep. My eyes slowly opened, and the back of my head was somewhat numb. The floor felt colder than a blizzard and rougher than a tree stump. After looking around the room I was in, I noticed something odd. I wasn't alone, which frightened me beyond belief. A man with a gigantic beard, larger than any beard I've ever seen before, was on the other side of the room, lifelessly staring down at the floor. After quickly observing him, I flinched, stood up and tried to run away. That was when I realized there was a wall blocking my escape.

In a complete state of panic, I clenched my fists and repeatedly smashed them against the wall, but the only noise I would hear was that of my hands failing to break through. My body and my sanity had lost all control. I kept extending my legs to make myself think the cell would somehow grow larger, even though I knew how ridiculous of an idea that was. I could tell that my fear of this cell was starting to overtake my conscience.

While I carried on with my never-ending tantrum of chaos, the old man remained still. He looked bored; it was almost as if he'd experienced this same situation in the past. But after twenty or so minutes, he finally looked up at me and mumbled, "You're not going to get out of here by doing that, so could you please stop?"

I was afraid to reply but I wanted answers, like any other human being would. Now tired, I slid to the floor and looked into the old man's eyes.

"Then what am I supposed to do?"

We were sitting on opposite ends of the room from each other, and it still felt like the old man was only a step away from me. For some reason, he had been giving off a frightening vibe. He could have been watching me sleep while I was knocked out and I found it difficult to control that thought. I was always alone in my bedroom when I was younger; to my knowledge, nobody had ever watched me sleep other than my mother.

The old man chuckled for a second and said, "You're probably new here."

I stayed silent.

"Is it your first week down in these caves?"

I was slowly growing more nervous, and I couldn't tell if the old man was able to interpret what I was feeling.

With a trembling voice, I mumbled, "Yeah... It's my first day," which was then followed by a brief pause of awkward silence.

The old man replied, "Wow—your first day. And you've already made your way in here?"

"I guess so."

The old man nodded his head and smiled.

After another brief moment of silence, I asked him, "So, where are we?"

Suddenly, the old man started to laugh. "It looks like you finally came to your senses."

What is he talking about? I thought.

He continued, "I'll give you all of the information you need, but I want you to bring me with you when you break out of this jail cell."

"What? What makes you think I'll be able to escape from here? I don't even know where we are."

The old man sat up.

"Isn't it obvious? You're a young man. You have strength. You have intelligence and perhaps even motivation. And I'm an old man. I'm sitting still and I'm already out of breath."

The old man wasn't making any sense to me. Yes, I was young, but that didn't mean anything to me. In my mind, I was still a weakling. Nonetheless, I couldn't say no; my hunger for information was already too demanding.

"Alright... Fine, when I escape this cell, I'll let you join me," I lied. "Now where are we? What is this place?"

With a satisfied voice, the old man exhaled and replied, "When the new prisoners come here from above, they're sent to a station where they get stamped. I think it's supposed to be a warning label, so if someone ever escapes this place, the outsiders know to stay away that person... But, of course, some people in this prison refuse to get a stamp, so they're sent here—a prison within a prison."

"Huh? Why would people avoid getting a stamp if it keeps them out of this jail?"

The old man squinted at me. "Well... Where's your stamp?"

I paused for a second.

"It's complicated."

The old man smirked at me. "We all have our reasons."

As the day passed, it felt as if the four walls restraining me from the other parts of humanity were closing in until I was crushed, along with the old man. He refused to tell me his name and continued watching me "try" to figure out a way to escape from this gloomy cell.

I noticed that each wall was made of a dark stone, as was the floor and the ceiling. There was also a small window which pointed at a distant brown rock, so it wasn't very appealing to the eye. The door which was all the way across the room from the window was where our food was served, because of a little flap which was just large enough for one of the guards to fit their hand through. The window was made up of four bars and it was decent in size; the rim stretched out roughly two by two feet, giving enough room for two people to look outside. I shook one of the bars, but the force of my palms didn't nearly have the strength to break it in half.

"Why don't you help me?" I asked.

The old man looked in my direction and asked, "What are you trying to do?"

I replied, "I'm trying to break the bars in half. They look old. Maybe you could help."

The old man chuckled and said, "I'm an old man—all weak and boney. The most I can do is sleep and complain."

"Complain about what?"

"There's plenty to complain about. I could complain about not being rich, about not having freedom, about the fool who's making a ruckus by shaking the bars on the windows—"

Not wanting to listen to any more of his complaints, I cut the old man off. "Say, how long have you lived in this cell?"

"Uhm… Almost six years," the old man replied.

Six years…

"What? Six years? How can you casually expect me to escape this cage if you spent the past six years trying to figure a way out of here?"

The old man didn't answer. Instead, he leaned his head back against the wall and muttered, "You know… Seeing that we've known each other for more than a day now, I might as well let you call me by some kind of name."

"What? That came out of nowhere." I replied dryly. "Although you bring up a good point, I wouldn't mind knowing your name."

"I wish I knew my name as well."

"You don't know your own name? Are you messing with me?"

"No, I… I can't seem to remember it."

What's with this guy? Seriously?

I looked back at the old man and said, "Alright, fine. If you don't have a name, then I'll give you one."

"Really? What did you have in mind?" the old man replied.

"Boney… Because you're as skinny as a bone."

The old man looked confused.

"Boney?" He said.

"Boney. That can be your new name."

"That name… It sounds strange."

"Well, that's the only one you're going to get from me. I'll either call you Boney or 'Old Man', so pick your poison."

After a brief pause, he replied, "Alright then. My name is Boney."

I smiled even though I was still confused. "Nice to meet you, Boney. I'm Charles."

I knew it was nighttime when one of the guards from the hallway yelled, "Go to sleep! Don't make us come in there and beat you again, Cook!" at one of the other prisoners. So, I only assumed that it was nighttime. Boney fell asleep within a few minutes and I stayed awake. I heard a bunch of voices coming from the distance. A shadow was now on the other side of the door, loudly echoing through the emptiness of the hallway. I could see the shadows because of a torch that was on the other side of the window in the cell door.

After a long night, I opened my eyes and whispered, "Is it morning already?" before realizing that a shadow was here to deliver breakfast. I could hear the guard fiddling with a stack of spoons and bowls on the other side of the locked door, grumbling about something unimportant as I waited to eat. I tapped on Boney's shoulder, quietly waking him up.

"Today is the day," he mumbled.

"Huh?" As usual, I had no idea what he was going on about.

"Find a way to attack the guard when he uses the flap to give us our food. Come on… let's get out of here. Today."

My voice grew louder. "Are you insane?"

"Shhhh! He's right there."

"No!" I whispered. "I'm not looking to die right now. I haven't even been here for a full day yet. And I'm hungry!"

"We can eat later. This is your chance to escape."

"I said no."

From the other side of the door, I heard one of the passing guards mumble, "Hey, hurry up with breakfast delivery. We have a floor meeting in ten minutes."

The guard who oversaw our breakfast delivery replied, "Alright, alright, I'll meet you upstairs in like five minutes."

As the passing guard walked away, Boney continued, "Come on, Charles. This is it. We're alone with the guard. Please... I'm begging you. Try something. Anything!"

"I'm not trying to get beaten—"

He cut me off. "I don't want to die here. Not here... Anywhere but here... Please, Charles. I don't want to die a dirty caged rat who's slowly rotting away in solitary. I'd spend the rest of my afterlife regretting my wasted life and all the things—"

"Oh my god, fine!" I whispered. "Just... Just stop with whatever point it is you're trying to make. I'll try something. Just... Give me a second to think."

I knew I was being illogical, but I couldn't listen to anymore of the desperation coming from Boney's mouth. For some reason, his words were saddening yet aggravating enough to make me force my hand. So, with what little confidence I had, I planned to grab the guard's arm, yank it back and forth as fast as I could, and hope to knock him out while also being able to reach the small set of keys that would most likely be jiggling from his belt. However, when the guard took the first bowl of "soup" and put his hand through the door, I stood still; in my mind, I was too scared to do anything. So, when his arm retreated into the hallway to grab a second bowl, Boney whispered, "Come on—this is your last chance."

"I know, I know," I replied.

I've only been here for one day... Is it really worth it? If I fail, then what? Will they beat me? Or will they kill me? I thought.

The guard put his hand through the flap once again and placed the second bowl of soup on the floor next to the first.

I can't believe I'm doing this...

Without hesitating, I grabbed the guard's arm and felt it struggling more than a trout that was snatched from the bottom of a lake.

"You got it!" Boney exclaimed, his echo bouncing off the stone walls. "Come on, Charles! Free me from this cage, my boy!"

A river of sweat streamed down the side of my head as I yelled, "Old man, if you get me killed because of this, I'll make sure to come back up from hell and haunt you for the rest of your goddamned life!"

After mindlessly struggling to get a good grip on the guard's arm, I finally took control and pulled it toward my chest, where I forced the guard's head to bounce off the cell door. I could then hear him drop onto the floor, along with the set of keys that were dangling from his belt.

There's no way that worked... I thought. *Surely this is some kind of trap.*

Even though an apprehensive cloud travelled down the back of my spine, I reached past the flap which was supposed to deliver our breakfast and struggled to reach the keys.

"I can't reach," I said.

"You're almost there—try harder," Boney enthused.

I pushed my arm to its full extent and somehow touched the keys with my fingertips, pushing them off the belt loop and into my palm. Once I got a hold of the keys, I was able to reach the lock and open the door from the other side.

"Oh lord! I'm free, I'm finally free!" Boney whispered with awe.

I peeked into the hallway, making sure no guards were watching our cell. It looked empty, so I turned back to the old man and whispered, "Let's go, before we get caught."

We ran out of our cell and turned a corner. It looked like none of the guards were monitoring the hallways, so we barged through the exit doors and made our way back into the caves. Then we ran. We ran far enough to the point where we could say that the cell we were once locked in was "over yonder". But after travelling in the same direction for what felt like three hours, I looked down at Boney and found him leaning against a rock.

"Boney, are you alright?" I asked.

He didn't answer. Perhaps he was too tired to speak.

"Boney?" I asked again.

He still didn't answer. The old man looked lifeless.

"Boney, what's wrong?"

I dropped to my knees and began to listen to his heartbeat.

4

A year had passed since the night of our escape. I remembered the night vividly for a few months afterwards, but then everything grew blurry. I knew I carried Boney to a hospital or some kind of medical tent; I didn't struggle too much, mostly because he weighed about a hundred pounds. The night at the hospital was short, knowing that the authorities wanted me and Boney back in solitary, if there really was some sort of authority down here anyway.

Since that night, I wore long sleeves and so did Boney because we never got our stamps. Nobody ever asked to see our stamps after that night, though, so the whole situation never became a problem.

Thankfully, Boney was just having heart palpitations. When we left the hospital, I joked that the excitement from his newfound freedom had driven the old man close to a heart attack. Since then, Boney and I lived together in a small hole we referred to as "our house". We called it that because our hole was a small part of a series of similarly sized holes that ran through the caves, almost as if we were a part of an ant colony. In this neighborhood, robberies were useless because every robber would get robbed themselves and the cycle would repeat. Food was difficult to obtain at the local "market" because there were barely any jobs being offered at the time, which meant that trading with the locals was our only option for getting food. Most of the jobs which were given inside the prison were mining related. When mining, the workers didn't have access to tools. Holes were dug with hand-made gadgets or those that were sold at the market. For the groups who were especially poor, they used other rocks to bang on the sides of the caves, hoping for a small scrap of precious metal to fall into their desperate hands. I know all of this myself because I was the rock bottom of the poor.

One day, I was on my way home from the mines, tired, worn out, and disappointed by the fact that the mines had yet again left me high and dry. Even after a full day of work, I couldn't find a stone that would cover the value of a single grape.

I stopped by the market with the little endurance I had left in me and searched for anything that I could bargain for. A crowd of people, around three hundred or so, surrounded the market area on what seemed like a busy afternoon. I stumbled upon a table which was selling fruit and stared at the pile of glorious apples towering over me. The shopkeeper glanced at the small set of stones I had in my hand and frowned.

"Hello," I said.

The woman moved a bucket of shiny stones from the ground to the top of the table.

She said, "Wanna buy something or are ya just gonna stare?"

I slammed three minuscule stones onto the table.

"What can I get for this?" I asked.

The woman fiddled with the garbage I'd given her. She rubbed them, smelled them, licked them, scratched them with another rock and once again, frowned at me. She placed them back onto the table and looked to her right where the line of fruits stood, adjacent to the butcher's table.

"Get out of here," the woman muttered.

I looked down and mumbled, "I see, sorry to bother you," and left the table in sorrow, knowing that I wouldn't be eating dinner again that night.

After yet another disappointing day, I got home and broke the news to Boney that we couldn't afford dinner for the night. He did not seem surprised.

"It's quite alright, you'll just have to work harder tomorrow," Boney said.

"I doubt I'll have the energy to work tomorrow," I replied.

Boney held out his hand, "Can I look at the stones you found in the mines today?"

I was confused yet intrigued. Boney always held this vibe to himself which unexpectedly changed from time to time; nobody else on Earth had this sort of appeal, if you can even call it that. Although, that may just be a personal feeling I have.

"Sure," I replied.

Boney took them from my hand and said, "Thank you."

"Why do you want to look at them?"

Boney threw the stones far into the distance. After the mixture of fog and mist disintegrated my day's work, Boney yawned and said, "try again."

"Hey!" I exclaimed. "What the hell was that for?"

Boney chuckled and said, "Now you can get the thought of failure out of your head. You have tomorrow and I can promise one thing."

"And what's that?" I replied.

"There are other stones in these caves and one day, one of them will belong to you. A big, shiny diamond, glimmering in the light. Or maybe a ruby, redder than the blood moon on a cool, October night."

Silence grew from the walls like a slippery rainforest vine. I didn't know how to reply, which probably meant that I agreed with Boney. I could feel my stomach praying for a single piece of meat or bread or something, but sorrow didn't help my case, nor anyone's case for that matter. Boney laid down against the wall, waiting for the next day to arrive and I joined him. I slept on the other side of the room.

"You know what, Charles? I never got the chance to tell you about my past. I know how we talked a little bit about our lives before we came here, but we never got down to the specifics," Boney mumbled.

"Isn't that a strange thing to bring up now?" I replied.

"Perhaps."

Does he even remember much of his past? The old man doesn't even remember his own name. I thought. *Actually… I shouldn't question it. After all, it's not like he's a typical person.*

A minute of silence followed. Then I said, "Alright, let's hear it."

Once again, we grew silent and I could hear Boney's breath from across the room, slowly seeping into my ears.

"It all started thirty years ago. I was a young construction worker who lived on the edge of the woods bordering the city. I had my dreams like everyone else—big dreams."

What kind of cliché is this? I thought. *But then again… I don't want to argue; I'm too tired. I'll just go along with his story and hopefully fall asleep.*

"Did those dreams come to fruition?"

Boney yawned again. "Nope. The big city gave me my chances and I tried to take the opportunity, but nothing worked out. Acting was my number one passion and I worked until the final bone in my body was sore. I even managed to get the star role in this incredible play which, for the life of me… I can't remember the name of."

Is he serious? That... That doesn't seem to make any sense to me. How can he be so amazed by something he doesn't even remember?

I replied, "So if you managed to star in a play, why did you say your dreams never came true?"

"Eventually the show itself faded away into nothingness. The audience didn't seem to like it," Boney said, now resting his head on a dirty beige rag.

"That's a shame."

"It is. I managed to stick around until the show was cancelled, though. For those few days of fame, I felt like a king. But shortly after, I got arrested. The police ended up sending me to a train station on the edge of the woods where I used to live, and a few hours later, I found myself down here."

"I'm sorry to hear that."

Boney ignored my last remark and continued, "I'll never forget the words the guards said to me when I got onto the train."

"What were they?"

"The guard said, 'I saw it—your show; it wasn't too bad.'"

That doesn't really sound like a compliment you should take to heart.

"So, why'd they arrest you?"

"I couldn't adapt. No, I *refused* to adapt. I enjoyed the acting business, and I thought I could get a second chance, but society went against me. So, when my agent fired me, I felt like I'd had enough. I couldn't take anymore loss, so I beat him to near death with my left shoe."

Then he giggled and said, "He was an annoying man. A real green lemon, rotting away in suite 5404... God, I hated that studio."

After Boney closed his eyes, I laid back and whispered to myself, "What the hell does any of that mean?"

As the silence between us grew thicker, Boney whispered, "Good night, Charles."

"Good night," I replied.

That was when another voice unexpectedly said, "Hello?" from the inside our house.

5

The voice sounded light and familiar.

I looked to my right and Boney was safe against the jagged wall opposite the entrance of our home. When I turned to my left, I saw a shadowy figure leaning against the entryway. I immediately jumped up from the ground and grabbed a sharp rock out of my back pocket, as if it were any better than a knife.

The shadowy figure walked past the entrance and became visible. It was that schoolteacher who I ran into a year earlier, Miss Annabelle, bathing in the light of a nearby torch.

"What are you doing in our house!" I screamed.

She took a step forward and started, "Sorry to scare you, but I'm here—"

I interrupted her, "Wait... I remember you."

Miss Annabelle looked away from Boney and replied, "And I remember you too. You're that Atara I ran into some time ago. What are you doing here?"

"What? What kind of question is that? I live here," I said. "What are you doing here? In my home? In the middle of the night?"

"Oh, so you live with my father?"

"Your father?"

"Yes—I wanted to see my father again after seven years, and it looks like he's under your care."

Seven years? I thought.

This had been the first time I'd seen Miss Annabelle in a year and there was just something about her that I couldn't explain, like the vibe Boney had given off when we first met. She hadn't changed very much from what I remembered of her, and I don't seem to remember her having an odd vibe back then.

With overwhelming skepticism, I got up and said, "And just how am I supposed to believe you?"

"What do you mean?"

"Do you think it makes sense for someone to casually show up at another person's house, say their roommate is your father who you haven't seen for seven years, and expect them to be okay with it? And by the way... It's the middle of the night!"

"Oh, come on! Don't we look similar? That should give it away."

"No," I said. "How'd you find us anyway?"

"I was passing by this part of town earlier today and I happened to notice an old man who looks just like my father entering this room with a younger man. So, I decided to stop by here after work, just to see if my mind was screwing around with me or not."

"So, you're telling me that after seven years of being separated, you just happen to find your father walking around? Just like that?" I replied in a sarcastic tone.

Then she replied in a serious tone, "Well... Yes."

"That seems too good to be true."

Boney was in the middle of sleeping when our conversation woke him up. With a soft mumble, he whined, "Charles, what is it?"

"Uhm... Apparently, your daughter came to visit," I replied.

He opened his eyes to their full extent and slowly got up, waiting to meet Miss Annabelle.

"Dad, you remember me, don't you?" Miss Annabelle asked.

Boney observed Miss Annabelle's clothes, her bodily structure, and her face. Her hair was tied in knots which stretched down the back of her neck. She was wearing a knee-length dress, except it was different from the previous one I'd seen a year ago. This particular dress had a specific design which consisted of white polka dots on a red background. The one I'd remembered from a year ago contained pink polka dots with a yellow background.

Boney had a hard time looking at Miss Annabelle, probably due to his poor vision. But to my surprise, he said, "Mary? Is that you?"

"Yes, it's Bloody Mary," Miss Annabelle replied.

You've got to be kidding me... And what kind of God forsaken nickname is Bloody Mary, anyway? I thought. *Surely this all has to be a dream.*

The room became awkwardly silent. I wasn't sure if I should have said something or not but either way, I knew that after this get-together, there was going to be some kind of strange outcome. I could feel it. After standing still in silence for about a minute or so, I saw Boney suddenly constrict Miss Annabelle in a big bear hug, clamping down on her as if she were a pearl in a clam. When Boney hugged her, I was surprised. That was the first time I had ever seen Boney willingly touch anyone besides me.

"Boney, you know who this is?" I asked.

"Of course—she's my daughter. She was separated from me some time ago. But now the skeleton is finally reunited with its skull!"

This is all a dream... I thought. *Seriously. It has to be.*

I was now in shock. Boney never mentioned anything about him having a daughter.

"So, where'd the name 'Bloody Mary' come fr—"

Boney let go of his daughter while she cut me off, "That was something we did when I was little."

"And nobody else knew about this?"

Boney joined the conversation. "Yup. Her mother left us when she was very young, so this was something we did to bond."

I felt too tired to continue this sudden conversation; I was far too confused, and my body craved sleep.

"Why don't we go to bed and continue whatever this is tomorrow? After work, of course," I offered.

Boney and Miss Annabelle simultaneously replied, "Alright," and chuckled while I tried my best to fall asleep.

I was on my way to work the next morning when I passed a peculiar sign. It read "Atara" across the top. I remembered the definition of that word. When I'd entered the caves for the first time, Miss Annabelle had called me an "Atara". Over time, I had figured out that "Atara" is part of the word "Atarashi"—a Japanese translation of the English word "new". Atara were the newcomers to the caves, so the term made sense to me.

Under the picture of the word "Atara", I saw an arrow, pointing to the train station where all of the newcomers were sent for their stamps of approval, or whatever else they were supposed to signify.

As I passed by the sign, I whispered to myself, "I've been down here for an entire year, and I still don't understand what the hell is going on."

I was now at work, ready to explore the cave systems for the thousandth time.

"Another day, another disappointment," I sighed.

From a few feet away, a deep and sturdy voice replied, "Wow—that's a depressing thing to say."

I turned around and a large six-foot-three man was towering over me. His skin was darker than the night and he was made of nothing besides rock hard muscles. He wasn't holding any tools, and I had surely never seen this man around the mines before.

"Wow you're big," I said in a joking yet partially terrified voice.

The tall man didn't laugh with me—he had a straight face that was made of stone. Once I stopped laughing out of fear, he took a step closer to me; we were now nose to nose.

"I guess you don't... get the joke," I said, stepping back. "It's because you look taller than anyone I've seen in this prison, so..."

And that was when I stopped talking.

The tall man took another step towards me, however I was now flat against a wall, almost touching lips with a stranger who had the strength to throw me back to the surface with the tip of his pinkie finger.

Suddenly, the tall man broke out laughing.

"I... I don't understand," I mumbled.

The man put his arm around my neck and playfully grasped my shoulder. "Why'r you so serious? I'm just joking around!"

"Uhm..."

Of course, I remained silent and confused, so he continued, "Oh, come on—don't you have a sense of humor?"

Amid my growing embarrassment, I cleared my throat and decided to change the subject.

"I've never seen you around these caves before," I said.

"That's because I just arrived," the tall man replied. "The name's Griff, just in case you wanted to know."

"Nice to meet you… Griff. Welcome to hell," I replied.

"And what's your name?"

"Charles."

"Charles! That's a great name!"

"I mean, I wouldn't call it a great name, but I guess—"

Without listening to the rest of what I had to say, Griff looked down and hugged me tighter than a snake wrapping around a man's neck. I could tell he was thanking me for acknowledging him, even though I could barely breathe.

After introducing myself to Griff and spending the day trudging through the caverns with him, I noticed that there was only one hour until the workday was over. I didn't come close to finding something good and neither did Griff. Even though he was just as unlucky as I was, Griff seemed to enjoy himself.

I continued digging in the same spot as yesterday and hoped my hard work would eventually pay off. But any form of profit seemed impossible. I couldn't afford tools, and as always, I had to do the handy work with my bare hands and a sharpened rock. It was very difficult to look for valuables without a pickaxe, but what else could I do?

By the end of the day, my pockets remained empty, and yet again, my disappointment was immeasurable. I didn't want to apologize to Boney two days in a row for doing my job incorrectly. However, before leaving the mines to go back home, I decided to continue digging for a few more minutes. At this point, I didn't care if I was able to buy an orange or even a single grape; I was desperate. Even the seeds of a pumpkin or a lemon would have pleased me.

"Anything interesting?" Griff yelled from a different hole.

"Nope, nothing!" I replied, loudly yelling across the mines.

But right at that moment, I was able to contradict myself. The tip of my pinkie finger felt a hard stone clash against it. After dusting the top of it off with my index finger and a pool of spit, I saw a peculiar rock staring back at me. It may have been small, but it was glowing brighter than a torch—it was incredibly fluorescent and beautiful in the dim light. I ripped it out of the ground and scrutinized it, amazed by what I had found.

6

When I left for work the next morning, I took the red stone out of my pocket and looked into its glimmering body. I was close to the market area and felt relieved that Griff was nowhere in sight. I never told him about my findings from the previous night because I didn't want to make him jealous.

I entered the market area grasping the stone with full strength. After walking around for a good ten minutes, I stumbled upon a small table adjacent to the entrance of the market. A short, raggedy man was on the other side of the table, glaring at me as I stared back at him. He was tapping his finger against the tablecloth, annoyed by the lack of business around the front of the market.

Eventually, I strolled past the other tables near the back of the market. The whole time, I found myself staring into my hands; they were clamping the stone even harder now. People could tell I was hiding something which made me seem like a thief, but I didn't care since I was only planning to run in and out of the market anyway. After circling around the area, I found myself now standing in front of the raggedy man whom I'd just passed; he was wearing a gold chain necklace and had hair growing downwards like a group of vines in the jungle. The man looked into my eyes, wondering what I wanted from him. Seeing that my clothes were covered in mud, along with the scratches and scars I had running past my arms, the man looked away, believing I had nothing to offer him.

I decided to break the silence and asked, "Hel—"

The man cut me off and replied, "You're too poor to buy anything from me. Go away."

Well, on any other day, you'd be exactly right... I thought.

"Actually, I've got something you might li—"

The man cut me off again and exclaimed, "You got something to trade?"

"Yes. Yes, I do."

I unclamped my hands and showed him the stone. "I found this in the mines, and I was wondering what it might be worth."

The silver trader snatched the stone from my hand and forced his right eye against it. Suddenly, his pupils dilated, growing larger than the earth itself.

"So, what's it worth? Is it a good find?" I asked.

"Yeah... It's good find." The seller was clearly in awe. "I haven't seen one this big in a while."

"So, will you buy it?"

He nodded his head and continued giving his full attention to the stone.

Even though I had no idea how much it was worth, I said, "Can I get a bucket of silver for it?"

I saw the fire of a thousand torches from a block away; the lights were all pointing in the direction of my stone. Their reflections shone away from its center and into the silver trader's eyes. I was now taunting the man, finding his weaknesses, and using them to my best advantage. I could tell the immaculate jewel he was grasping had more value than I'd expected, leaving an astonishing new personality I had created from pure luck. The horrific rivers of greed were unexpectedly creeping into my veins, but it felt wonderful knowing that the silver trader was now my puppet.

"Hmm..." the man mumbled.

I knew that my offer was unfair. An entire bucket of silver could have easily fed ten families; both him and I knew that. But in the eyes of the trader, the rarity of the stone felt overwhelming. I knew that the silver trader, as money hungry as he was, would have loved to keep this stone for himself, either as a hypnotic clock for future gem-collecting customers, or a show piece to justify his rank among the other local traders.

Finally, the trader tucked the stone away in his pocket and shook my hand. "Alright it's a deal."

The next day felt different from the usual struggle of hard labor. A pile of silver was overlooking the doorway to my home and a bucket of vegetables stood in the center of the room—a rarity which was birthed by my newfound wealth. Soon enough, Boney and Miss Annabelle woke up. I didn't know why she was still staying with us, seeing she had her own home, but I didn't really seem to care anymore. For some strange reason, I felt like she was growing on me.

Once Boney opened his eyes, I could see the utter shock on his face when his eyes grew to the size of the sun.

"What... what is this?" Boney asked; his face was blank.

"I finally got lucky," I replied.

Miss Annabelle's excitement didn't grow to the length of mine or Boney's, but she was still visibly amazed. One morning, our house was nothing but hole in the wall, and the next day, it was as close to a mansion as we could possibly get. Eventually, the dirty rocks and once-jagged walls disappeared since they had been replaced with wood. Everything was cleaned to the bone, so much so that the floor started to sparkle. The doorway was now arched with concrete and our sleeping quarters were made of feathers and fur instead of solid rock.

Towards that week, Boney sat down next to me and asked, "How much of that silver have you spent so far?"

"I don't remember. But don't worry, we still have plenty to use," I replied.

I reached into the bucket of vegetables sitting near my bed and picked out a fresh bright carrot. As I took a bite, my taste buds congratulated me. Boney joined me and so did his daughter. For Boney, biting into a cucumber was the first time in weeks he had been able to taste real food.

The next day, I left the house and ended up in the center of a nearby town. I didn't need to go back to the mines for at least the next month, so I refrained from working. Instead, I spent my free time wandering around, curiously exploring the caves and what they had to offer.

Funny enough, my first stop in my transient journey of freedom was a newspaper stand. This was not because I wanted to see what kind of things the captive reporters down here were writing about, but because I saw my face pictured on the front of one of their newspapers. It was titled: *New Entrepreneur Sells Rare Stones.*

What's this? I thought.

As I walked closer to the newspaper stand, the tall and muscular woman running it immediately noticed me.

"Oh, you're that rich stone seller everyone's talking about," the newspaper lady exclaimed.

"No, I wouldn't call myself—"

Another man who overheard the woman talking cut me off. "Wow, you really are that man in the newspaper!"

A wave of attention suddenly started to whirlpool around me. I was now the cause of a crowd gathering around the newsstand.

I whispered to myself, "Oh no."

The newspaper lady exclaimed, "Where'd you find that red diamond? Do you have any more of them?"

I wasn't sure why everyone was so concerned over the diamond. After all, it was just one stone—a result of pure luck. It was *my* luck. I wasn't planning to share my prosperity with these random strangers. At least, that's what I thought they'd wanted from me.

Even though my nerves were getting to me, I tried ignoring the crowd over my left shoulder and asked the lady, "Could I get today's paper?"

"Of course," she exclaimed. "That'll be ten pieces of silver."

"What? Lady, are you insane?"

The woman running the stand glared at me. So did the growing crowd.

She's scamming me. I thought. *Did she hire these people to stand around just so I'd be forced to overpay?*

Ten silver coins equated to two large buckets of vegetables. I knew the price of the newspaper would be somewhat more for me, seeing that I was considered wealthy now, but I didn't expect this kind of outcome. It was clear that I didn't want to spend ten pieces of silver on a piece of paper, but if I didn't spend it, then I was afraid that the crowd behind me would turn into a riot. So, my decision was forced.

Without a moment to lose, I said, "I'll take it!"

7

The next day felt calm, even though it was no different from the others. All of my once-overbearing stress continued to slowly fade away, leaving me to finally take some control of my own life. After waking up in the middle of the day, I looked over at the silver pile; it looked much smaller than the prior day, but I still wasn't worried. The house looked just a little more beautiful than it was before and Boney was enjoying himself on the small wooden balcony which had been constructed overnight. I stepped onto the balcony while Boney was reading a book, one that I wasn't familiar with.

"What's that you're reading?" I asked.

"I'm not too sure. The book doesn't have a title," Boney replied.

"What? That doesn't make any sense. Let me see what you're reading."

Suddenly, Boney closed the book and asked, "Do you think we'll ever be able to leave this place?"

"That was sudden... What do you mean?"

"This prison. Do you think we'll ever get out of these caves, Charles?"

I didn't know how to answer. For the past few months, the thought of escaping these caves fled my mind because I was too busy mining. At the time, my purpose was to keep myself and Boney from starving to death.

"How come you're always asking me these sudden, random questions? What are you trying to get out of them?"

"Just answer the question, Charles."

I exhaled and replied, "I hope so."

After a brief pause of somewhat awkward silence, Boney said, "I hope so too," and went back to reading.

What was that all about? I thought.

After that strange interaction, I left home and walked into a local bar. But when I found myself surrounded by a flock of strangers who were looking my way every five or six seconds, I realized that this wasn't any typical bar; it was a casino. The front door was older than the wrinkles under Boney's eyes and the walls were made of granite. The air was thick with smoke and hundreds of grimy wooden tables were all around me, scamming people into thinking that they would become rich over the course of five minutes.

I walked up to one of the tables and approached the man standing behind it. There was a red knife on the table; I assumed it was there to prevent thieves from stealing from the casino. As I looked at the man, he didn't return my gaze. He was trying to peek into my pockets instead. They were filled to the brim with silver.

"Gonna make a bet?" the man asked, before giving me a small piece of paper and a tiny pencil along with it.

I looked at the scrap and the pencil, wondering why he had given these to me.

"Bet on what?" I asked.

The man looked confused, thinking I'd been here before. From the clothes I was wearing, one could have guessed that I frequented the place.

"You place a bet on who you think is gonna win the game," the man said.

I was still confused, so I asked, "What game?"

"The volleyball game."

I remembered volleyball before getting pushed into this prison; it was an alright game. I never thought that I'd bet on it but seeing that I had some money to spend, why wouldn't I? In the distance, I was able to see a cracked-up stone field and a tall gray net towering over the athletes who would play their live games.

"Oh... Sure, I'll bet three of my silver coins on blue," I said.

The man chuckled.

He said, "Oh, come on, boy. That's pocket change!"

After hearing those words, I became hesitant. But even so, I raised my wager and said, "I guess I can raise you another five."

Suddenly, a woman in the crowd behind me yelled, "Oh, c'mon you cheapskate, bet some real money!"

I turned my head and thought: *is she talking to me?* Then I looked in my pockets and realized that I didn't have many coins left.

Should I pay more? I thought.

If I win, I'll double my money. Otherwise, I'd lose a few more days' worth of food. The outcome is fifty-fifty...

Oh, screw it.

"Alright, I'll give you thirty coins because that's all I've got," I said.

My stupidity didn't get the best of me; it was now controlling me. The man behind the counter looked surprised and eagerly took all of my silver. He didn't leave the slightest speck of dust in my pockets and was now looking at the field, crossing his fingers that blue would come to its downfall. However, after waiting an hour for the game to end, the man from the counter came out of the back room with a pleasant smile on his face.

"Well, who won?" I asked.

"Didn't you see? The red team dominated," he replied. "Better luck next time."

"What... Did you say red team w—"

"Sorry bud. Come back tomorrow—maybe you'll win your money back."

I couldn't believe what I was hearing. I'd lost all my money—a quarter of my fortune— all in a single day.

How could this happen? I thought. *Am I that much of an idiot?*

When I got back home later that day, I saw Boney on the balcony, reading until his eyes would burn off from exhaustion. Miss Annabelle was cooking something that smelled heavenly, but at the same time, she looked depressed. I wanted to ask why, but then I looked to the side of the room where our silver pile used to be. It was all gone, so I started to panic.

"What... What happened to all our money?" I asked.

"Greed got the best of me. I spent the last of our funds on land," Boney murmured.

"Land? What land?"

"Well... there was this salesman who came by. Long story short, I bought a big chunk of private land from him. It was an impulse decision..."

Miss Annabelle stayed quiet and continued stirring tonight's dinner in the frying pan.

"We should be fine, though. You still have those fifty coins on you, right?" Boney asked. "Or was it thirty?"

I wish I could have said yes, but I'd ruined myself by walking into that treacherous hell of a casino. So, I looked down and Boney could see my empty pockets in full view. He walked back to the corner where he always rested and fell asleep, knowing that sooner or later, we would go back to our old ways of poverty.

With my last droplet of sanity, I looked at Miss Annabelle and asked, "That smells good. What are you making?"

She replied, "Something that will be a reminder of how you and my father screwed yourselves out of all your money."

"Me and your father?" I said. "How come you weren't there to stop him from giving all of our money to that salesman?"

"I was at work, what was I supposed to do? While I was out there making money, you two idiots spent the day giving it all away."

I took a seat on the balcony and exhaled. After only two weeks, I couldn't believe that this meal was the final remainder of our food supply. I looked through all of our baskets and found nothing; not even a crumb was left behind. This was the last day of our beautiful wealth.

The next morning produced had already felt dreadful. I woke up, full from the night before, and rubbed my eyes in a begrudging attempt to wake myself up. That was when somebody knocked on the door.

"Who comes knocking on people's doors this early in the morning?" Miss Annabelle whined.

"No idea," I replied. "It's probably a beggar or something. I'll tell him to go away."

I got up and opened the door to find a short and shadowy woman standing in front of me. She was wearing a fancy black suit and glasses larger than a set of stars. She was also half the size of Boney, and had the face of somebody who had never smiled once in their life.

Why is she wearing a suit? I thought. *Aren't we in a prison? How'd she even manage to get something like that down here? It's so clean...*

"What do you want?" I asked.

"Are you Charles Balkin?" the woman replied.

I was surprised to hear her use my full name. Nobody had called me Charles Balkin for years and suddenly, a little woman whom I'd never met decided to walk into my life and blurt out something so hidden. Even Boney didn't know my last name yet.

"How do you know my last name?" I asked.

"That's private information," the woman replied.

Who is this woman?

She was wearing a name tag which wasn't really a formal name tag. It was just an old piece of paper with her name haphazardly written onto it: Mrs. Gloria Jamison.

"So, you're married, huh?" I asked.

She ignored my last remark and said, "Hello Mr. Balkin, I'm Mrs. Jamison."

I exhaled and replied, "Again, what do you want? And why are you wearing a suit with a nametag? This is a prison, isn't it?"

Mrs. Jamison handed me a crumpled sheet of paper, of course with messy writing, stating, "Charles Balkin, you have found a rare diamond in the mines which you have worked in. The rule for working at the mines is such that if a stone worth more than ten silver coins is found, fifty percent of the earnings must go to the prison."

"What the hell is this?" I asked, now frustrated.

"Those are the rules, sir."

"These rules were never mentioned to me."

"They most likely were. Didn't you go to the Atara orientation?"

My eyes widened.

"Of course…" I lied. "I just—"

"So, then you must have slept through the rules."

As I looked at Mrs. Jamison, a river of sweat seeped from the side of my head.

"Well, whatever the case, it looks like we're going to have a problem," I said.

"And why's that?" Mrs. Jamison replied, now with a stern voice.

"I'm broke. All my silver is gone."

She glared at me and muttered, "Hmm… That is a problem."

After a brief moment of silence, I said "Well, since I don't have any money… bye!" and started to close the door.

Suddenly, Mrs. Jamison stopped the door with her right hand. She retrieved a black pistol from her left pocket with her other hand and said, "You're in debt, Mr. Balkin. You and your belongings are now a possession of this prison."

8

Another year passed and it felt much, much slower than the previous one. I still never had the chance to fully pay back my debt to Mrs. Jamison and life was worse than ever. I lived in a small corner of the mines with Boney, knowing that everything had been taken from us. Food was just as difficult to obtain as gold or serenity. Griff never knew about my entire "wealth phase" and for the two weeks I hadn't arrived at the mines, I'd told him I had a serious fever, which he believed. The public, including the newspaper, quickly forgot about me. I was a public interest for a couple of days and the second I lost it all, I was known as that one part of history which will always be ignored.

Boney was sleeping in a small crater which wasn't very visible to the naked eye. Miss Annabelle hadn't visited for a week she was busy teaching her students. I was just a regular worker at the mines now.

Griff walked up to me, about to start his day's work.

"Ready?" Griff asked.

I can't believe I still don't have a pickaxe. If I wasn't so stupid, I would have bought one when I still had all that silver! I thought.

I exhaled and replied, "Let's get at it."

Griff didn't know where I lived, and he didn't know about Boney. Occasionally, he asked where my other friends were or if I had any in the first place. All I ever said to him was, "Oh, them? They're at work," or something like that.

Three hours of the workday had soon passed. I was at my regular mining area, adjacent to Griff's. I didn't expect anything to change today for me or Griff, but I still had some hope of finding a stone that would make me some money.

As I continued to mine with a lousy flat rock, a thought came into my mind.

Has anyone ever tried to mine their way out of this prison? If we're allowed to mine whatever we want and wherever we want, then surely someone managed to find a hole to the surface. Right?

When I asked Griff about it, he said that he wasn't too sure. But when a more experienced prisoner overheard our conversation, he butted in and told me that some of the old prisoners who found a way out ended up getting tortured or shot on the surface.

The next week I returned to work in the mines. After two hours of accomplishing nothing, I ended up fiddling with a few worthless rocks I'd found the day before.

I stood and mumbled to myself, "Back to work," before picking up a sharp rock which acted as my "pickaxe" and jamming it directly into the wall. For the next few minutes, I continued plowing through dust until a tiny ray of light suddenly caught my eye. I had never seen such a bright light in the mines before; darkness always destroyed the sensation of light in these mines.

Oh damn... Did I dig into someone's home again? I thought.

I started removing some of rocks from the area in front of me, all because I wanted to see what that diminutive ray of light meant. As my eagerness to work increased, I began mining faster out of pure curiosity for what that light might be.

Suddenly, the wall in front of me collapsed. As a storm of dust quickly consumed my body, I heard Griff running into my mineshaft.

"Charles!" He Yelled.

When the dust settled, he found me resting on a pile of rocks.

"You alright?"

"Yeah," I replied, getting up and pushing two or three fist-sized rocks off of my body. "I'm fine."

I looked past the mountain of fallen stones and dust and realized I'd run into a small cave. After most of the dust cleared, we stood up, coughing from all the particles flying through the air.

Griff pointed his flashlight at the small cave I discovered and said, "Wow, you found a cave."

"Is that rare?" I replied.

"I've never found one before so maybe."

I brushed even more dust off my clothes and asked, "Do you think this cave's worth exploring?"

"I'm not sure," Griff replied. "Let's find out."

The cave was very narrow so there wasn't a lot of room to walk, especially for Griff. He was taller than any man I'd ever seen before, which made it difficult for him to fit in between the walls. Nonetheless, Griff was still somehow able to keep up with me. As we made our way towards the end of the cave, I saw the small ray of light from earlier; it was slowly growing larger.

"I don't see anything valuable in here," Griff said.

I could hear his echoes bouncing off the walls all the way from across the small room, even though Griff was about twenty steps behind me. After taking another few steps forward, I entered yet another cavern which was smaller than the other, except this one had a bright pulse of golden light shining directly through the ceiling.

"Hey Griff, I think I found something!" I yelled.

Griff crawled into the room, struggling to adjust himself with me inside of the room as well.

"Wow… That looks like sunlight," he said.

"I think it's coming out of a small hole from really high up," I replied, jumping to see if I could reach the source.

But of course, Griff was able to touch the hole.

"Give me something hard," he demanded.

I gave him my mining rock and he smashed it against the ceiling, causing an avalanche of dirt to rain down onto us. After the dirt rain subsided, Griff said he felt a piece of metal or something of the sort stuck to the ceiling.

"Can you dig it out?" I asked while shining my tiny flashlight at the ceiling.

"I'll try."

As Griff hammered at the metal plate stuck into the ceiling, I cheerfully yelled, "Is it coming off?" while bringing the flashlight closer to the ceiling of the cavern.

He was pulling on the metal *thing,* but nothing was working.

"What could a bar of metal be doing in here?" I asked.

"I think there's more," Griff replied.

"What?"

After dusting off more of the ceiling, Griff revealed a two-by-two meter window that was stuck into the ground. We were under it; on the other side, I could see the sun, grass, and all the other parts of nature I'd missed so dearly for the past few years.

Wait… what's that? I thought. *Is that grass?*

"Oh my god," Griff whispered, his eyes growing and his jaw agape.

"We found a way out of here... Out of this prison..." I mumbled. "Was it really that easy?"

The metal window was a door to heaven.

9

I was now running through the mine shafts, searching for Boney and Miss Annabelle who said she would visit today. The jagged walls of the cavern made a slanted, narrow tunnel, forcing me to crawl through the rest of the exits. I knew I was overreacting and shouldn't give away our position or our new discovery, but this was our only chance to escape the prison, especially for Boney, who had lived in these caves for the better part of a decade. I recognized where I was and found myself sprinting just to get closer to Boney. When I got home, I found him waking up as I ran into our hideout on the side of a small cave system. Miss Annabelle was quietly talking with him, but I abruptly interrupted them.

"Boney, the outside! We found a way out!"

A flood of confusion overtook Boney's face, along with Miss Annabelle's.

"What do you mean by that? Is everything okay?" Miss Annabelle asked.

"We found a way out of this prison!"

Boney and Miss Annabelle looked at each other. At first, they didn't believe me, perhaps thinking that I was trying to pull some sort of confusing joke.

"You should gather your things. We're leaving now," I said.

"Wait a minute, Charles," Boney replied.

"Right now."

Boney repeated, "Wait."

"Oh, and don't forget to bring the water canisters," I continued.

"I think you're rushing thin—"

I cut him off and said, "Just trust me, Boney."

As I grasped his shoulder, Boney replied, "I've been down here for over eight years, Charles, and not many people have come close to escaping from this prison. Not to mention, everyone who's escaped in the past was probably killed. You can see why I'm a little hesitant about this. Are you sure whatever you found isn't some sort of trap?"

I never thought about that... What if that window in the ceiling is a trap? I thought. *It does seem odd that there's a random window stuck into the ceiling of some small cavern in the middle of nowhere... And why would it lead to the surface? No... No, that wouldn't make any sense! Why would someone make a trap in some random cavern? It's in the middle of nowhere. Surely, this window we found has to be a coincidence of some sort... Maybe it's part of some kind of sewer system or something? Oh, whatever! That doesn't matter right now. We saw grass and leaves and sunlight; that's what matters. Wherever we'll end up, it won't make a difference because we'll be out of here!*

In a much lighter voice, I replied, "Please, Boney. You have to trust me on this. I know it's sudden, but... you just have to trust me on this."

Boney looked at Miss Annabelle and thought for a moment. Finally, after deciding their fate, he replied, "Alright, I'll pack. It's not like we have very many things anyway."

Within twenty minutes, Boney and Miss Annabelle started to gather their things. We only took what was important to us: old clothes, a few water bottles, and a pair of old sunglasses I'd stolen from the "lost and found" bin at a local market.

Minutes later, Miss Annabelle urged, "Alright, I'm ready. Let's run," while walking out of our home.

I agreed and followed Boney out the door, but as we abandoned our hideout, a certain poster which was hanging a few feet from away us suddenly caught my eye. It said, "Wanted: Charles Balkin and 'old man'. Reward: four ounces of silver."

Boney's picture was next to mine.

When I saw the poster, I grabbed Boney by his shoulder and pointed at our photos. "What is this?"

He was as lost as I was.

"I don't know…" He replied. "I've never seen it around here before."

"Surely this is some kind of joke."

"Well… maybe not. I'm guessing the guards down here still remember our escape from solitary," Boney replied. "Although that was two years ago."

I turned to Boney and asked, "Are you talking about the jail cell? How would anyone even remember that?"

"Yes," He replied. "Either that, or Mrs. Jamison is still looking for us. We owe her twenty pounds of silver and we've missed our last six payments… Or perhaps it was seven."

"None of that should matter," Miss Annabelle interrupted. "If you did find a way out of here, then screw Mrs. Jamison and screw that jail. None of that should matter anymore. Now let's go; we might be in more trouble than we think if we stay here."

We agreed with Miss Annabelle, knowing that if we were caught, Griff would be the only one of us to escape this place.

Thirty minutes had passed since we ran away from our home. We were now hiding behind a giant red rock near the threshold of the mines and watched as the prisoners holding their worn-down tools marched forward for another day of work. As all the prisoners entered the mines, I noticed someone who was holding a poster with my face on it. The word "wanted" was printed in bold over my head.

I whispered, "Hey, look at that."

Boney turned his head and saw the poster. He replied, "Another one?"

"What's going on?"

Miss Annabelle stepped into our conversation and whispered, "Shh... You two are being too loud."

Suddenly, a man about ten steps away from us spotted Miss Annabelle's head behind the rock, poking out. At first, I wasn't sure if we'd been discovered or not but after a crowd of three or four people quickly formed around the rock, I realized the growing severity of our situation.

I pulled Miss Annabelle's arm towards my body and said, "Dammit, I think they saw you."

She pulled her arm away from me and whispered, "Are you sure?"

I poked my head out from the rock and noticed that the crowd of four people grew into a crowd of six.

With a nervous voice, I replied, "They definitely saw us."

After a brief pause, Miss Annabelle looked at Boney and said, "Everything should be fine. Nobody knows that you're my father so nobody will suspect me of being a fugitive like you two."

With some sarcasm in my voice, I replied, "I've always wanted to be called a fugitive."

Boney ignored my previous remark and replied, "Yes, but when somebody from that crowd comes behind this rock to see who we are, they'll notice us."

Miss Annabelle thought about something for a moment and then smiled as if she'd come up with a brilliant idea. She said, "Fine! Since nobody knows that I'm related to you and Charles, I'll just come out and make up some excuse for why I've been hiding behind this rock... I'll say I was taking a nap."

Boney chuckled and replied, "And how do you know that everyone will trust your explanation without checking what's behind this rock first?"

I butted into their conversation and said to Miss Annabelle, "You're overthinking this. I have a much simpler solution."

"Which is?"

I replied, "Sprint."

Miss Annabelle shook her head and said, "Sprint? My father is in his mid-seventies. He can't sprint. And that's dangerous! What if they catch us and turn us in for the reward?"

"Uhm..."

Boney stepped in and agreed with my plan. He said, "It's our best option. Originally, I thought it would be a good idea to tell everyone about your discovery, Charles. That way, everyone would follow us out of this prison and we wouldn't have any problems since we would all be free. But nobody would trust us. Everyone would think we're petty liars who are trying to bluff our way out of being turned in for the reward. Honestly, I think running would give us the best chance of getting out of this situation."

Miss Annabelle grabbed Boney's arm and whispered, "But dad, you can't run."

"I'll be alright, honey. We don't have to run far. I'll make it, I promise. I'll even hold your hand so you know I'm always next to you."

A few seconds passed. Then, with a great deal of hesitation, Miss Annabelle replied, "Alright."

"Good. Now, once the clock in the center of town rings, we'll make a break for it," Boney said, getting ready to run for his life and freedom. "It's almost noon so we'll only have to wait for a minute or so."

I nodded at Boney and so did Miss Annabelle. We were ready. There were now ten seconds until we ran. The crowd built up, which was becoming a growing concern. Soon, there were about twelve people in front of the rock; perhaps some were waiting for a friend to join them in the mines... At least, that's what I'd hoped. *Nine, eight, seven, six.* Five seconds left sweat running down the sides of our heads. *Four, three, two, one. Click.* The clock was now ringing, and it was time to execute our plan. We ran past the riot of our fellow prisoners, along with the rock. It took the crowd a second or two to realize who we were and that we had escaped them, which is why they stood still in the midst of confusion for some time. But soon after, they began to run after us, realizing that we were the people from the wanted poster.

As we entered the mines, Miss Annabelle let go of Boney's hand and stole a pickaxe that was leaning against a wall within the entrance of the mine. Without a second to spare, she banged it against the top of the entryway and then dropped it. As she continued to run on, an avalanche of large rocks blocked anyone from leaving or entering the main parts of the mine shaft for at least the next few minutes, or until the cleanup crew would come along to remove the rubble.

I yelled, "Good thinking!"

Miss Annabelle smiled and replied, "Just keep running!" even though she was out of breath.

We were sprinting will all our might and it was difficult to stop because we were panicking, knowing that a lifetime of imprisonment was just one step behind us. Eventually, after enduring the worst sprint we'd ever gone through, Miss Annabelle and Boney followed me into the cave which I had discovered and where Griff had been waiting. Miss Annabelle and Boney didn't know who Griff was but when they had first laid eyes on him, they were forced to look up high, stunned by his overwhelming height. I was pretty sure that the expression they made was the same one I made when I had first met Griff.

Miss Annabelle started to block off the entrance of the cave while Griff continued struggling to break the metal hatch.

"I think somebody from the outside has to open it," Griff exclaimed, beginning to worry. "I've been trying to open this thing for over an hour now... This damned thing just won't budge."

Griff turned around and noticed two strangers. He asked, "Who'r those two?"

I pointed at Boney and replied, "That's Boney." Then I pointed to Miss Annabelle and said, "And that's Boney's daughter, Miss Annabelle."

Griff smiled.

"It's nice to meet the both of you. I'm Griff."

Boney smiled back and replied, "Likewise." Miss Annabelle then followed suit. After everyone had gotten acquainted, Griff looked around and decided to take a break.

We were sitting in a circle in the center of the small cave watching Boney start a fire with two rocks and some dried-up leaves which had fallen through the ceiling. In the meantime, Griff wanted to lay down in the tunnel which led us into the cave because of his height. Within minutes, a large fire sprouted into the air while each of us sat next to a pile of rocks, ready to use them as weapons just in case we were discovered.

As the fire crackled on, Boney decided to make some conversation. So, he said, "Why were you three sent here as prisoners?"

That's an odd thing to ask right now. I thought. *But whatever; I'll play along.*

Miss Annabelle was the first one to speak. She replied, "I was born down here so I don't have a choice," she said, leaning back against a wall.

"Where's your mother?" I wondered.

"Who knows?" Boney said. "She disappeared two months after my dear Mary's birth. I don't really remember much about her anyway."

"Wait…" I replied. "How's that possible if you were only down here for eight years?"

Boney looked confused. "Eight years? I haven't been down here for eight years…"

I scratched the back of my head and continued, "No, you told me you've been down here for eight years!"

"No," Boney said. "It's definitely more than that… maybe around twenty or so years. Maybe more. Maybe less."

What the hell is he talking about? I thought to myself, now more confused than ever. *You know what, I'll just ask Miss Annabelle her age.*

But before I could reply, Boney continued, "What about you, Griff? Why'r you in here?"

Griff thought for a moment and replied casually, "I killed a farmer and all fifty of his sheep."

Everyone in the room moved back and simultaneously replied, "What?"

Griff chuckled. "I'm joking… My god, ya'll are easy to fool."

We all joined in with some form of uncomfortable laughter and dropped our anxiety, returning to our spots around the glowing fire.

"So why are you here, Griff?" Boney asked.

"I stole some clothes."

I replied with some confusion in my voice, "And that's it? That doesn't seem like a good reason for throwing someone in prison."

"Certainly. That sounds ridiculous," Miss Annabelle added.

Griff rolled over and said, "You're right about that."

After his words echoed, a sudden wave of silence flooded the room. I could feel a cooling gust of wind fly out from the metal hatch. The Earth itself could have been taunting us but we had been taunted for so long that it didn't affect us. As the breeze grew stronger, a leaf fell through one of the bars in the metal window and landed on Boney's lap. I could see his face glow red behind the golden fire. Boney tightened his fists and the leaf crumpled into a pile of nothingness. Once a new leaf flew through the ceiling, the crumpled parts of the old leaf flew out of Boney's hands and landed back onto the surface of the Earth.

We lost our topic of conversation because all we wanted to do was stare at the fading sunlight through the space in the metal window. But when I got up and walked closer to the ray of light, a shadow suddenly appeared over us, blocking out the sun entirely. A gloomy figure leaned down and stared at us as if we were a newfound species.

<u>10</u>

Somebody was standing over us above the window; someone short and skinny. Boney crawled back against the wall and Griff instinctively stood in front of Boney in the corner of the cave. As the sun moved through the sky the figure's face turned visible. She had long hair, dirt all around her legs, and a bright green dress resting on her body. She looked down at us and we hesitated to talk to each other, mostly because we were awestruck. I looked around and nobody was planning to break the silence.

Finally, I said, "Hello…"

The woman leaned down.

"What are you four doing down here in this disgusting hole?" the woman said.

Boney started to talk, "We were…"

Griff cut Boney off, "We're miners, except for this old guy…"

"Very funny," Boney muttered under his breath.

"We used this metal hatch to get down into the mines. I guess it managed to fall back down while we were working and now, we can't get out," I lied, following along with Griff's plot.

That sounds believable… I thought. *At least, I think so.*

"Oh, I see," the woman replied.

I didn't know what to say and from here on, so I let Griff do most of the talking. He seemed to know what he was doing.

"Do you mind opening the hatch for us?" Griff asked.

"Not at all! But I don't have any tools," she replied. "By the way, my name's Aria, just in case you wanted to know."

Aria looked somewhat innocent because of her plump cheeks which were a significant contrast to the dark color of her hair. She was pretty and seemed nice too; nothing about her seemed off-putting to me. At least, that was the feeling I had gotten from her.

As Aria thought about the situation, she started to scratch her head, wondering how to free us from this jail. Once silence seemed to fill the air again, an idea flew into my head, although it ended up being more of a risk than anything else. I thought of re-entering the mines and retrieving the pickaxe that Miss Annabelle had dropped by the entrance. However, I wasn't sure if Griff would let me go back.

"Would a pickaxe be able to break the lock on that thing?" I asked.

Griff started, "Charles, you're not thinking of going back in—"

But he was cut off by Aria who replied, "I don't see why not. A pickaxe looks like it should be enough to break this lock."

"Alright then, I'll be right back," I said.

"I don't see a pickaxe down there with you," Aria replied.

"I left it back in the tunnel. Give me ten minutes and I'll bring it back here," I explained.

"Alright, well, I wouldn't spend a long time trying to search for it or else the tunnel could collapse on you," Aria pointed out.

I chuckled and replied, "Don't worry, I'll be fine."

Boney understood that I wasn't doing this for myself, but Griff couldn't accept my fate; he looked incredibly hesitant, clearly not wanting me to go.

"Ten minutes," I said, leaving everyone to wait for my return.

Griff looked down at me and said, "Be careful, you idiot."

"Don't worry—"

He pulled on my shoulder and whispered, "I saw those wanted posters of you on my way here, Charles… Seriously, be careful. They'll kill you if they have to."

We nodded at each other, hoping for a miracle to befall us in the next ten minutes.

I left the cavern and my paranoia grew. The workday seemed to be almost over. Not many people were mining anymore, but I could see a pile of tools wallowing behind a muscular man who was slamming his pickaxe against the wall beside the entrance to the mines. The pile of tools was only ten, maybe twenty, steps away from my current position. I saw another crowd of workers leaving the mines, tired and worked up. After watching him mine for a few minutes, it was clear that he wouldn't leave, which made my situation even more terrifying. I didn't have the time to wait so I had to compromise. After looking around for some sort of attempt at a disguise, I took a handful of dirt and threw it onto my shirt. Then I rolled around in a small pool of mud and covered my face. After transforming myself into a monstrous recreation of the man in front of me, I casually walked up to him; he was now staring at the wall, seemingly tired. The pile of tools behind him looked like it was all his.

I tried to change the tone of my frightened voice and asked, "Hey, do you mind if I borrow one of your pickaxes for a few minutes?"

The man turned around, looking calmer than I thought he would be. He stood up straight and looked me directly in the eyes. Finally, I saw him move his lips.

"Why do you want my pick? You gonna steal it?" He questioned, leaning closer toward my face.

"No, of course not! Mine broke and most of the other guys left already—"

The man cut me off and said, "Alright, you know what. Cause you're so desperate, I'll give you five minutes and if I don't get this pick back by then, I'll beat you to hell."

"Yessir," I said, shaking more than the leaves on a tree during a hurricane.

"Five minutes," He continued. "Not a second more."

That was easier than I thought...

"Understood. Thank you."

"Take it," he said, pushing the smallest pickaxe he could find into my chest.

To an extent, I was surprised by the cooperation of the man, probably because of how nervous I was. The problem now was to avoid the other miners while on my way back to the cavern.

So, I headed back, thinking that we were as close to freedom as we'd ever been. However, when I was only a few tunnels away from Griff and the others, an annoying, stubby man suddenly noticed me walking back into the depths of the mines, so he decided to walk up to me and think that he could "help me" by cleaning me up.

"Excuse me, sir, but you seem to be covered in mud. I can help you clean up if you'd like," the man said.

"No thanks. I'd rather stay like this," I replied.

"No, really, it's my job. Please, let me clean you up a little."

"Really, I don't—"

"No charge!"

Before I could respond, he grabbed a bucket of salty-green water that he'd been carrying around with him and dumped the contents all over me, from head to toe. He could see that I was holding a pickaxe and the salt may or may not have ruined the shine of the metal, but that wasn't the problem. What truly bothered me was that when the man saw my face, he seemed to recognize it.

"Wait a second…" The man whispered to himself.

I shushed him, but that made the man only talk louder.

He continued, "You're the guy on those wanted posters! Charles Balkin!"

Dammit! I thought.

"You're that guy! The one whose face is all over this mine!"

"No! You're mistaking me for someone else. Seriously, just leave me alone."

"Sorry, bud. I need the money."

He started to call some of the other miners over, but I didn't give myself into loss. Instead, I had to use sheer force.

One of the other miners yelled, "Yeah, that's him! There he is!"

There were now five miners standing between me and freedom. I knew I didn't have enough strength to deal with them, so I had to flee—flee and surpass them. I was sure that by now, my five minutes had ended, and the miners weren't my only new enemy. So, in my final attempt to escape this God forsaken hell, I passed a corner and ran faster than I ever did in my life. The crowd behind me had now become a riot.

I turned another corner of the mineshaft and found myself about twenty steps away from the smaller cave where my friends waited. I thought that I would make it. But when the giant man who lent the pickaxe to me suddenly jumped in my way, blocking the entrance to the cavern entirely, everything started to fall apart. At least, I thought so until I noticed something peculiar about him. There wasn't a red stamp on his arm.

11

The man who'd given me the pickaxe had a tattoo across his arm. The letters were giant alongside a group of black dragons and strange demon-like creatures, spelling out "Victor," which was most likely his name.

As I stared at the giant in front of me, one of the men in the riot behind me yelled, "What are we waiting for? Come on, let's turn him in already!"

I purposely looked toward the cave where the others were hiding, and Victor saw where I was looking. Hopefully, I wasn't making a mistake. As I looked back at Victor, he grabbed his pickaxe out of my hand, firmly grasping the wooden handle which was dark enough to be mistaken for coal.

"Hey," I whispered.

Victor grabbed the neck of my shirt with his other hand and said, "What?"

"You're not going to turn me in, right?"

He chuckled. "Give me one good reason why I shouldn't turn you in?"

I have to come up with a lie—something that'll get me out of this, I thought.

A brief wave of silence followed Victor's question.

That's it! I got it!

I said, "Victor? I imagine that's your name… Do you know why I'm wanted?"

He rolled his eyes and replied, "Get to the point."

I lied, "It's because I found a way out of this prison. The guards down here don't want me telling anyone about the escape route, so they put a bounty on my head. In fact, I'm on my way down there right now, so join me."

"That's a pretty bad story you came up with," he said while chuckling. "I don't like liars, you know."

I was desperate, so I begged. "You have to trust me... Please... The escape route is right around the corner."

"Don't start crying. Be a man, you little rat."

A tear ran down the left side of my face, and as I stopped it with my thumb, I whispered, "It's the truth. On my family and on God, we found a way out of here. That's why the people running this place are getting desperate to find me. Why else would they be posting my face on every crack and corner of this prison?"

Victor stood still like a skeleton. He couldn't decide between the reward or seeing whether or not I was telling the truth. This situation had quickly grown into a gameshow; Victor either got the chance to win enough food to last him a month, or choose the mystery box and gamble for a better reward. I looked into Victor's eyes and they looked clueless, whiter than the clouds above the metal window.

"I get it," I continued. "This whole situation is high risk, high reward for you. But you have to trust me, here. The reward is—"

He cut me off and muttered, "Shup up and give me a second to think, would you?"

Finally, after a full minute of contemplation, he made his decision and chose the mystery box. Victor knew where I wanted to be because of the looks I'd given him. Every few seconds, I looked at the tunnel to my right and I knew that Victor was able to follow my line of vision.

Our eyes were locked, so much so that they were slowly merging into one form of vision.

I heard Victor exhale and mumble, "I'm gonna kill you if you're lying to me. I really am."

Without warning, he threw me into the entrance of a nearby tunnel and ran in after me, slamming his pickaxe against the ceiling of the tunnel entrance. This caused yet another avalanche, forcing all the stone above the entryway to crumble and separate us from the rioters. I could hear a storm of now infuriated voices from the outside, cursing at us with nothing but fury in their hearts.

"That was one hell of a risk I pulled for you," Victor said, getting up as a mountain of dust cascaded down his body.

I took the tool from his hand and said, "Thank you."

Then I started to walk away when Victor said, "Ay! Where are you going?"

"Just follow me, I'll explain on the way," I replied.

And that's exactly what I did. I told him about Aria, the girl we had just met who was going to free us, and Boney. I told him about Miss Annabelle who had never even seen the outside before, and that she was Boney's daughter. I told him about Griff and how Aria shouldn't know anything about the prison, or the fact that we were prisoners. I told him a story that we'd go along with when we got back to the cavern with everyone else. I would have to say that I found Victor in the tunnel; he had gotten lost in the mines because this was his first day on the job.

As we got to the small cave and joined the group, everybody looked at us; they were excited and confused. I told our made-up tale to Aria and the others decided to go along with it, knowing how close we were to getting out of this prison. So, after finishing my questionable but probably good enough on-the-spot story, I handed Aria Victor's pickaxe and she got to work. After waiting a good ten minutes or so, we heard a slight cracking noise which came from the hatch. It turns out that instead of unlocking the lock in the hatch, Aria had destroyed it completely. But of course, nobody had a problem with that. Soon after, she helped us all up one-by-one, however multiple people needed to lift Griff because he weighed more than a block of iron.

I was the final one to escape. Griff grabbed both of my hands and lifted me out of the cave with ease. We were finally free. As I took my first step on the grass in what felt like decades, my bare feet started to tingle. Any shoes I'd previously owned had been taken away to pay my debt to Mrs. Jamison, so I was still getting accustomed to walking around barefoot. As I looked around, I saw a tear drop from Boney's right eye and seconds later, his left. In contrast, Miss Annabelle looked unbearably confused. It's quite ironic that a teacher like Miss Annabelle had never even seen a tree or grass up close even though she was teaching her students about those sorts of things for several years.

As I looked at the sky, I was blinded by the light of the sun. I hadn't experienced this kind of harsh light for a long time and neither had anyone else. After looking around in awe for a bit, we all decided to walk around and explore the surrounding area. This made Aria look at us as if we were patients in a psychiatric hospital, but in the moment, nobody seemed to care. I wandered off and found a family of moss sitting on top of a small hill which, for some reason, made me feel wealthier than a prince. I felt freedom and the pride of overrunning the tyranny of the guards and Mrs. Jamison's debt.

Boney walked up to me and said, "We should leave soon, just in case any guards find us out here."

"What do you mean?" I asked, "We're in the middle of nowhere. Why would there be guards waiting for us all the way out here?"

"You never know," Boney replied. "That hatch in the ground probably has some kind of purpose, and that purpose might be related to the guards who dragged us into that prison in the first place."

He made a fair argument, so I nodded and replied, "Good point. Let's go."

I looked over at a set of unfamiliar mountains and saw a couple of houses in the distance which were sitting in the middle of nowhere. They were made of red wood and the grass surrounding them was greener than an emerald in the sunlight. At that moment, everything felt peaceful.

"What are you four waiting for? I'll take you all to the train station so you can go home!" Aria yelled, running along the river. It was quite large, but what really amazed me was the color of the water; it was glistening brighter than the skin of a pearl. The serenity of the water was almost trance inducing.

Aria eventually led us past the river. She started to scale the mountain, meaning that one of us would end up having to carry Boney. The hills were jagged, and the stones were like the spikes of a porcupine on our bare feet, a detail that Aria seemed to ignore. The mountains didn't seem to be very tall, but they were definitely tall enough to cause a sweat. It seemed to grow hotter as we got closer to the top because of the intensity of the sun out in the open. A river of sweat quickly formed on my forehead; it spread to the rest of my body within minutes.

As we continued up the hills, I heard a grueling sound from the top of the rise.

"Did you hear that?" Miss Annabelle yelled, turning to me and Boney.

I agreed with her. I heard some strange cry from the top of the mountain which almost sounded like a hoard of angered bloodhounds, or a working tractor being set ablaze in the middle of the night.

"This isn't the first time that the mountains have made these sounds," Aria replied.

Miss Annabelle asked, "What are they?"

"I don't know. In fact, nobody knows. All we know is that they're treacherous, but we've gotten used to them," Aria said.

"It sounds like a bunch of rabid dogs barking," Griff replied.

Aria replied, "There's a prison not too far from here, so that noise might be coming from guard dogs. I'm not too sure, though..."

Nobody replied to Aria's comment. Instead, we kept on scaling the mountain, which wasn't as difficult as I thought. Although, it might have been more difficult in Griff's case because he had volunteered to carry Boney.

After struggling up the mountain for a while, we reached the summit. In the distance, we could see an immense city; it was much more developed than the small desolate town back on the other side of the mountain.

"Why is such a desolate little town hiding from this city? Your home is so close to this place," I said.

"I enjoy the serenity up here. Whenever there are too many people living around me, I don't know what I'd have to be dealing with," Aria replied.

"At least the view's astounding," Victor said.

The city was almost larger than the caves we'd just escaped, possibly even larger. It was shaped like a circle, and it was surrounded by a long mountain range. In the very heart of the city, I saw a tall building which overlooked the others. It was made of a bunch of vast quartz pillars, gold, and other materials which were difficult to find in the caves. All the other buildings didn't seem to stand out as much.

"That must be the town hall," I said while pointing at the building.

"Really? I thought that building was a courthouse," Griff replied.

"You four like to guess, don't you? People around here like to call that big building 'The Palace'," Aria said.

"That makes sense," Victor said. "That place definitely looks like a palace."

Griff was carrying Boney for so long he had forgotten to put him down.

"Can we go inside?" Boney asked.

Aria stared at the structure and wouldn't let her eyes off the sight. When I looked at her dress, I noticed she had the same design imprinted on it as the symbols I'd seen back in the caves.

"I wish. They stopped taking visitors ever since... Actually, I don't remember when they closed off entry, but I know guests were once allowed inside," Aria said, looking uncertain.

"Who's 'they'?" I asked.

"The authorities. I don't remember who manages them—nobody in our town does, at least to my knowledge."

"Oh, I see."

After gazing into the distance for a little while, we started to descend the mountain, entering the vast city. I was surprised by the fact that not a single gate guarded any of the homes or shops, aside from the palace which was very heavily guarded. As I passed through the streets, the authorities were checking people's arms, searching for something very specific.

Aria pointed to one of the guards and mumbled, "Look over there."

One of the guards was searching a person's arm. Suddenly, the blue-uniformed policeman who was conducting the search called in for backup who then raided the person. One of the men stole a rope from somebody's house and fiercely tied the poor fellow's hands behind his back.

"Please," He yelled. "Have mercy! Let me go! What did I do?"

As the squadron of guards passed us, I saw a red stamp on the man's hand. It was a stamp, no different from the other stamps in the caves. He must have been a former prisoner of the caves who had also somehow found his way out.

I turned away from the entire incident and thought to myself, *Damn, that was brutal.*

Suddenly, Aria exclaimed, "Hurry or we'll miss the show!" and ran toward the palace.

"Show? What show?" Victor replied.

Aria didn't hear Victor but assumed we would follow her, which we did. Thirty steps later, we ended up in a crowd which was bordering the outside gate of the palace. A line of authorities was circling the crowd, keeping a keen eye on every person who entered the perimeter of the building and its gate.

Eventually, we caught up with Aria who looked astonishingly excited. A metallic podium was standing in front of the main entrance to the palace which was still locked. The crowd started to grow larger, and larger, and larger. Moments later, the crowd began to cheer as a man from inside the gate started walking out the main doors. He wasn't as physically strong as Griff but seemed to have more power over the public than anyone else around me. He was wearing the fanciest clothes I'd ever seen: a suave leather coat, touching the ground with a pile of fur sticking out of the back, and gold-crusted glasses which gleamed back at the sun. The man's hair was very long, and he was wearing a red hat which was the most noticeable thing about him. The red hat was also made of fur, which was sticking out of the bottom, surrounding the top of his head. It was still easy to notice the man's hair though because it grew down his neck like a carpet of snakes slithering down a tree in the jungle.

I whispered, "Aria, who is that man?"

"That's the president," Aria replied.

"So, doesn't he control the authorities?"

"Well, he always said in his speeches that he didn't enjoy violence and that he left one of the other staff to take full control of the authorities."

I didn't believe that statement because it seemed illogical to me. How could a president not have control over his own guards?

As the president approached the stand, he demanded that all of us listen. He cleared his throat and banged a set of cards against the surface of the podium.

"Hello, my loyal citizens. I see all your colorful personalities which unite to listen to the problems we face today," the president exclaimed.

He paused and took the first card on the top of the platform and shifted it to the bottom of the stack. I looked over at Victor and for some reason he looked angry.

"Victor, are you alright?" I said.

"I'm disgusted by that… that *thing*, sending poor children into a prison and taking away their rights," he replied.

"Him? How do you know that he's the one sending people into that prison?"

"I remember him," he said. "I remember his face and his hair and that stupid red hat on his head. He's the one who locked me up in that prison."

"Wait… So does that mean this is your hometown?"

"No," Victor replied. "He probably moved cities and became president here after sending me away."

I could tell Victor was livid. His hands were shaking, his forehead was scarlet, and he seemed to be hyperventilating.

"Just calm down. We're free now," I reminded him.

"Yeah… Sure."

Victor seemed to calm down as I looked away from him, directing my gaze back to the president.

"As we continue advancing our society, we must remain keen on eradicating the criminals and the scum from our population. We must stop violence from entering this city and every other city in this great country," the president continued.

Victor tightened his fists; his fingers were pale.

"First of all, due to recent events, I have decided, along with the other staff of our palace, to move the curfew from midnight to eleven," the president said.

The crowd started to murmur, suddenly discussing the new law. It was strange that if a new law was announced, nobody wanted to say anything. All anyone did around this city was mumble.

"If there are any complaints…"

The president was cut off as Victor suddenly barged past the crowd and leapt at the president.

From the crowd, I yelled, "Victor, what are you doing?"

Without a second to spare, Victor punched the president's nose about two or three times, causing a stream of blood to trickle down the president's face.

Griff yelled, "Stop it, Victor! What are you doing? You're going to get yourself killed! Stop!"

Miss Annabelle joined in and screamed, "Stop! You idiot!"

Chaos quickly ensued as a storm of guards flooded around Victor, separating him from the city's leader who was now covered in his own blood. Once the two were far away from each other, the president scrambled to his feet and exclaimed, "Send him to the dungeon; hang him!"

12

Victor was rushed past the golden gates that were guarding the palace, struggling as he desperately tried to free himself. I couldn't figure out the reason for Victor doing what he did but in the long run, it didn't matter. As I watched Victor enter the front doors of the palace, I realized his fate; he was a dead man. I don't like the image of someone dying after they've helped me, but what could I do? None of my thoughts seemed to matter at this point because minutes from now, he would be hanged without mercy from anyone in this city.

After the guards took Victor away, the president was rushed into the palace. When the door behind him closed, one of the guards walked back onto the podium. He was clearly infuriated, tapping his pointer finger harshly against the rim of the microphone. Then he stood up, straightening his back and raising his chin to make the civilians look like a crowd of ants from his point of view.

"Hello," He mumbled. "It's obvious that all of you think you're innocent in some way, watching a desperate fool bounce on our beloved president."

A pause of silence followed his words.

"If a tear is spotted in any of your eyes, that means you must have some sort of relation to this man. If so, you too will join the fool in his fateful execution," the guard exclaimed, taking out a black pistol and shooting it into the air.

A loud gasp grew from the crowd.

"Tomorrow he will be killed and then devoured by his own kind. The president will be expecting all the civilians who live in this city to attend the execution," the guard concluded. "If you don't choose to attend, you are welcome to join this fool in his punishment, along with anyone else who deserves to die."

That was the end of the guard's speech. He stepped off the podium and turned around. His back was now facing the crowd as he walked past the golden gates. They shut seconds after, causing the crowd to scatter. Aria was shocked, as was I, initially thinking that Victor had the ability to control himself.

"Well, he was right about one thing," Griff informed. "Victor is an idiot."

The next day was ticking down second by second, until the moment of Victor's execution. We were all sitting at a table outside. We never left the city because the borders had been reinforced by lines of guards who refused to let the civilians exit. The restaurant we were at was full, with every table taken; apparently there weren't many restaurants in the city. There wasn't much in the way of culture here either and the food seemed boring. Each of us were eating the same thing: cooked dough and strawberry jam. Nothing seemed interesting about this city except for the palace.

I cut a piece of dough with a dull knife when Griff asked, "So what's up with this place? Why are these guards making so much commotion over their president being tackled by some random outsider?"

Aria shushed Griff and replied, "Be quiet, or else they'll hear you."

Griff nodded and lowered his voice. "Fine. But why? It seems like all the guards in this city have two sticks up their asses."

Aria took a bit of jam and replied, "I don't know. It's always been that way down here."

After some awkward silence, Boney dropped his fork which landed softly on the rest of the dough on his plate. Then he mumbled, "After this damned execution is over, I'm leaving this place and going back to my old life."

"Do you mean acting? I thought you would've retired by now," I replied.

"Acting? Ha! The day I'd go back into that life is also the day I'd return to that prison."

Suddenly, after realizing Boney's mistake, I couldn't breathe. Boney didn't realize what he'd said until Aria's face grew confused.

Naturally, Aria looked at Boney and decided to ask what we were talking about. She said, "What prison? And what did you mean by acting? I thought you four were miners."

I didn't know how to answer her. Nobody did.

"Just an old occupation. It's nothing much," I replied.

She continued, "Were you a prison guard? Or were you an actor?"

"Both," I replied. "Boney used to be an actor and I used to be a prison guard. Now we're miners."

Aria squinted at us and then focused her attention on Boney. "What did you mean when you said you're 'going back to your old life'?"

Dammit, Boney! I thought. *What did you get us into?*

"It's an expression we use in the mines," Boney lied.

"What does it mean?"

"It... It means we're tired. After a long twelve-hour day of mining, we would always say 'I want to go back to my old life' as a group before going home.

It was obvious Aria didn't believe us, so Griff tried to change the topic of conversation by asking, "So, when does the execution begin?"

But Aria ignored Griff's question, "Alright, I want to know the truth. What's going on here? Why are you four lying to me about your lives? I thought we were friends. Friends don't lie to each other like this."

"What are you talking about?" I replied. "We're... We're not lying to you, Aria."

"Then why do you keep stuttering?"

I was silent. None of us knew what to say. Perhaps we were bad liars.

Tension began to increase as a guard walked by our table. He looked at us, so we all tried to relax. We weren't trying to cause a ruckus. However, once the guard left us to our conversation, all of that once fading tension quickly reignited.

"You know..." Aria continued. "If you accuse anyone of anything in this city, and I mean anything, you'll be searched to the final bone of your body until it collapses," Aria said, looking at one of the nearby guards.

Miss Annabelle tried to laugh the entire situation off and replied, "Aria, there's no need to make threats—"

"They're all very paranoid here; the citizens and the guards."

"Aria, please... stop jumping to conclusions—"

"It'd be a shame if all that paranoia were to suddenly be thrown onto you four."

This time, Miss Annabelle didn't say anything. So, Aria mumbled, "Really... It would be a big shame to see such a thing happen."

We looked at each other and fell into a pause of silence. As the tension between us grew denser and denser, Boney finally blurted out, "Fine! We're prisoners."

Oh no... I thought.

It was obvious that Boney's conscience couldn't take any more of the threats, so he decided to tell the truth. And so, as the tension among us slowly faded away with the wind, Aria relaxed. From the look on her face, I couldn't tell if she was worried since we were convicts or satisfied since Boney revealed the truth about us.

"Were you four charged with murder?" Aria asked.

"God no. To be honest, none of us really know what we were charged with," I replied.

"Well, if somebody says that they've been in prison for something in this city, they're looked at as if they're a criminal for the rest of their life. People really do overreact these days."

Now curious, I asked, "Why do you not seem surprised? And how can you believe that we're prisoners so easily? You're not even questioning us!"

She laughed a bit. "It's a well-known statistic around here that a third of the population in this city is imprisoned. So, I'm not surprised... Every week, the newsletter releases a new article regarding another escapee who'd been discovered by the guards. To tell you four the truth, I've met other escapees before. Some fled from this place, never to be seen again, and some got caught. Usually they catch most of them, but a surprising amount get away, which I suppose is good because most of the prisoners here have never done anything serious anyway." Then, in a much quieter voice, she continued, "If you ask me, the people who run this place are power hungry monsters. They want nothing less than a utopia, which is why they're trying to get rid of anyone who isn't willing to become one of the president's zombies."

I guess I shouldn't be surprised... I thought. *Given how big those caves are, it wouldn't make sense for us to be the first to escape. The rest of what she said also seems true to me. These guards are always running around, looking for something small to uncover. They're nothing but a bunch of mindless zombies who are desperately trying to send anyone and everyone to the caves or the slaughterhouse... As soon as this damned execution is over, I have to leave this place. We have to leave this place. I don't know where we've ended up, but it's surely not a city of freedom. If anything, this place is making me feel like I'm back in the caves.*

Miss Annabelle leaned into the center of the table and whispered, "You won't tell anyone, will you?"

Aria replied, "No. You four seem like nice people. I would never do such a thing."

She replied, "Thank you," and sat back in her chair.

Suddenly, the table grew silent. I could hear some of the conversations coming from other groups of people near the restaurant. They were all dull and mindless.

After the end of an awkward interaction between Aria and the rest of us, a large crowd gathered in front of the palace. This was a wonderful chance to break the silence, even though the event itself was most likely going to be disturbing. We just met the poor man about a day or two ago but it's obvious that freedom wasn't meant to be for him.

The crowd around the palace grew larger like a flock of robin traveling south, running away from the Northern Lights. The head guard who'd spoken the day before stepped onto the stage and began to introduce the president. I got up, along with the others, and joined the flock. The president was waiting for the head guard to step off the platform when everyone's attention shifted to the main doors of the gate. Victor was forced outside. His hands were tied behind his back; I saw them as he walked by us. They were as purple as grapes.

The head guard finally stepped away from the stage and let the president walk right past him. Everyone grew silent and looked over at the president.

Before the main event, the president was going to make a speech. He cleared his throat and banged his hands against the top rim of the stand to make sure everyone had their attention on him and not the poor man who was about to be executed.

"Hello, my fellow civilians," the president began, standing tall and proud. "Today is the day that we get rid of this man, Victor Sonsvin, and his horrid, disgusting crimes against the sacredness of our city."

Sonsvin? I thought.

Victor never told us his last name… He knew that death was unavoidable, so why would he reveal himself to the authorities?

"If you would, please look to the very front of the gate!" The president exclaimed.

I looked to the front of the gate where Victor stood. A rope was holding his chin, and his feet were standing still on a wooden platform which would open on the president's demand. Surprisingly, Victor was wearing the same clothes he'd worn in the caves, except now they were clean.

What happened in that town hall? I thought. *Why are his clothes clean? What did he see in there?*

The president stepped off the platform and looked over to the gallows, loudly exclaiming, "You may begin!"

_13_

Two lines of guards crossed paths. The president was now in command of the executioner who was more than ready to pull the lever. The fear in Victor's eyes was quickly growing.

"Before we kill this man for his crimes, does anyone have anything to say?" The president asked.

I was afraid to reply; everyone was. The tolerance for crime or even speaking out in this city seemed criminally low and I was just as close to being eradicated as Victor, except I chose to keep my mouth shut. Everyone in the crowd was silent; nobody had a single word to say. As I glanced at Victor one last time, I noticed he was staring back at me. That made me uncomfortable because if the authorities saw him looking at me in his final moments on this Earth, perhaps they would start questioning me.

"Well then, since nobody has anything to say about this man, we will—"

Aria cut the president off on his final remark and exclaimed, "This man is a prisoner, and he came with others!"

What the hell did she just say? I thought. _What is she doing?_

Had Aria betrayed us? In my mind, she was supposed to be a loving human being.

"I see. And where are those prisoners now?" The head guard asked.

Suddenly, Aria was frozen, refusing to say another word. She stared at the head guard with a clueless face, thinking about what to say next.

"Are you planning to tell us?" The president asked. Then, in a much grimmer voice, he continued, "Or are you lying in an attempt to push back this man's execution?"

"No… it's not that," Aria said, hesitant to go on.

The head guard turned to the president and asked, "Excuse me, sir?"

"What is it?"

"Do you think she's lying?"

"It seems like she is. Even so, I can't take any chances. I can't handle another bunch of criminals running around and committing treason in my beloved city," said the president. "And even if there aren't any criminals running around this city, she might know the man who attacked me, assuming her intentions here are to push back the execution by making up these desperate lies."

I started to worry about the trouble Aria had led herself into. As the situation worsened for her, I thought to myself, *Seriously, what is she doing? Did she try to give us up, only to back out in the last second? That might be it… I can't think of any other reason as to why she'd blurt out such a ridiculous thing. That is, unless she's trying to save Victor.*

As I expected, the president grew angry. So, with great hostility in his voice, he yelled, "I don't plan on waiting anymore. Guards, take this woman into the palace!" and pointed at Aria.

Suddenly, I stopped the guards and exclaimed, "Wait, I'm her brother! If she's going, I have to go too."

Miss Annabelle looked at me as if I was an idiot; she might have been correct.

Directly after my statement, the head guard glanced at the president and saw him nod.

"Fine," he muttered. "Do as you wish."

As the guards led us through the gates, I looked back and saw the executioner pull the lever, opening the wooden hatch under Victor's feet. Within those few seconds, the crowd dispersed as Aria and I entered the front doors of the palace. Boney, Griff, and Miss Annabelle were staring at me from the other side of the gate, unsure of what to think. In those last moments, I thought to myself, *it looks like Aria wasn't trying to save Victor after all...*

As we entered the palace, I was amazed. The walls were covered in gold and the floors were shinier than a safe full of newly printed coins, each one representing another lost soul in the caves. A giant chandelier which was showered in thousands of diamonds and silver parts was overlooking the main entrance. Large flames were sprouting out of the candles which stood on top of the diamonds and the reflection from the jewels glowed off the arches from the beautiful doorways.

There were a series of paths which could be taken out of the front room and each door in the palace was guarded. The head guard stood in front of us, waiting for something to happen, when the president walked through the door behind us. He stared at me and Aria in the eyes and waited to hear something from us. Anything. I looked at Aria who seemed embarrassed, either for not being able to keep a secret or something else that I just quite couldn't figure out. After waiting in the silence for a few seconds, the president walked past us and sat on a wooden stool.

The president crossed his legs and said, "Well?"

I had nothing to say. Whenever Aria had tried to talk, she would immediately look back down at the floor. So, the president continued to stare at us, never to mutter a single word in the process. Finally, I decided to kill two birds with one stone and break the silence while simultaneously trying to get Aria out of this situation.

"I'll show you where the prisoners are," I offered.

The president ignored my previous remark and said, "You look familiar."

I was now confused. "What?"

"Yes. I think I've seen you somewhere before."

What is this man going on about? I thought.

"So... are we not here because of the prisoners—"

"Hold on!" The president continued. "No... I was right! It's you! I knew it!"

After listening to the president's ambiguous back and forth mumbling, I became annoyed. So, with what patience I had left in me, I stood up and walked over to the president on his stool. As he looked up, I held out my palm and slammed it against his eye. After assaulting him, three of his guards ran into the room and held me back against the wall.

"It's quite alright, I deserve that for being confusing," the president laughed.

"What the hell are you people talking about?" I yelled.

Instead of acknowledging my confusion, one of the guards stood up and said, "But sir, your eye..."

The president cut the guard's sentence short. "Do me a favor and get the table ready. We have guests."

The head guard continued, "Are you sure?"

"Yes!" The president exclaimed. "Now hurry, I'm getting impatient."

Hesitantly, the head guard turned to his men and ordered them to fulfill the president's request. As the guards headed off, the president grabbed my left shoulder and said, "Follow me. You two can forget about why you were originally brought in here."

I stood and replied, "Wait, what's going on?"

The president ignored my previous remark and led us to the dining room. The napkins were folded delightfully, and several bottles of wine were splayed out on a large rectangular table which went from one end of the room to the other. A dark red cloth rested under each of the plates and a bunch of crystal glasses sat on top of the napkins, along with the forks and knives which were bordering a row of golden chairs that were sitting at the edges. Everything looked beautiful but I suspected that this was all for some kind of trade.

Eventually, we took our seats; the chairs were surprisingly comfortable. In the city, it seemed like only five or six dishes were served in each restaurant because of how dull everything here was. But in this small heaven of a room, lines and lines of different dishes filled the surface of the table; the sight was incredible. Surrounding them were all the other people who were visiting the palace. As I looked around, it was clear that they were all beginning to congregate.

"Who are all of these people?" I asked.

"People I enjoy having around. You know... The people who are on my good side," the president sneered.

As these fancily dressed elites sat in their chairs, Aria and I felt like we were the main attraction. Everyone looked at us like we were animals, almost as if we were a circus attraction. By now, I had imagined that the only reason the president wanted us around was because we knew who the other prisoners were. I couldn't think of any other reasons for us being invited here.

Everyone began with their meals once the bell rang. I thought I saw snails, a stuffed pig with a cooked red apple in its mouth, and, as mentioned by some of the other diners, a few bottles of wine which were apparently impossible to find in the city. Aria had told me about these bottles of wine while we sat down at the nearby dough and jam restaurant; she read all about them in a local magazine just the other day. As it turns out, the rarest of all the bottles mentioned in that magazine was right in front of us; it was called "Goodnight My Bleeding Rose". Aria said it was her favorite wine because after having just one sip, she'd already be half drunk. But now that I think about it, she might have just been a lightweight.

After scanning through the entire table, a sudden noise came from the stairs. When I turned around, I could see a man walking down them; he seemed like he was almost as old as Boney. His face looked very familiar to me and after thinking for a brief second, I knew who that horror of a man was. His name was Frederick, my father.

14

He walked past the stairs and sat at the edge of the table. The final seat of the dinner table was meant for the most important guest, which, strangely enough, happened to be my father instead of the president. In fact, the president sat right across from me; I was the one who was adjacent to the final seat.

Once Frederick sat down, the table grew silent; the guests were waiting for a speech. As I looked at my father for the first time in years, I recognized his dead eyes and his gloomy gray hair from a mile away. To me, his somber demeanor felt like the definition of despair.

My father clanked a spoon against his glass and watched the table freeze before his eyes.

"Hello, my friends," he exclaimed with a friendly voice. "All I can say is, thank you for all of these wonderful gifts: wine, meat, and all of these colorful fruits—they really are the rubies of the Earth."

Like you'd be thankful for something, I thought.

"Enjoy tonight's feast! Indulge and relax!" Frederick concluded as he raised his glass. "To me, becoming seventy!"

Everyone at the table started to cheer for Frederick. They clinked the tips of their wine glasses together and drank heartily. As an explosion of conversations among the guests suddenly broke out, my father looked at me.

Frederick took a sip of wine and said, "Well Charles, I see you finally had the luck of meeting up with me once again."

The president was listening to our conversation while sipping the most bitter wine I'd ever smelled. As I poured myself a glass, I ignored my father, mimicking what he had done to me throughout my childhood.

He continued, "I know you might be angry with me—"

Of course, I was angry; I was livid. So, I broke him off and mumbled, "You're a bastard."

"How can you say that to your father on his birthday? I can tell that prison may have not been the best place for you," he admonished. "But it was also necessary. You were becoming way too chaotic, especially after graduation."

"Seeing that you've been ignoring me for the past decade, I doubt you actually care about my wellbeing," I replied.

"No, of course that's not true. You are an interesting man, Charles. Sure, I might have been distant during some of your childhood, but to whom does it matter now?" Frederick asked.

"Why did you ignore me? And for Christ's sake, what did I do to you to be thrown into a prison?" I exclaimed, banging both of my fists against the table. "They were going to kill me, you know! If I missed that train, they would've shot me... You're own son! And you don't even care!"

I had frightened Aria and the president by the level of my voice. Within seconds, the entire table grew silent. I had created a scene, destroying all the other conversations along the way. Since I didn't know what to do at this point, I had followed in Aria's footsteps; I looked down at the floor and ignored everything around me until things grew better. After a minute or so of awkward silence, the conversations between the house guests picked up again.

"I'm sorry," he replied. "I just needed everyone to leave me alone for a little while. I had too much to do. I was stressed."

I giggled and trembled with anger at the same time. "Really?"

"Yes," he said, trying to sound sympathetic.

After a second of silence, I asked, "So, why didn't you let me out of that prison? Why did you keep me there for two years? To me, that doesn't seem like 'a little while'."

Frederick grew silent. Aria looked up, now interested.

"Come one," I said. "It's a simple question."

As I expected, Frederick continued to remain silent, so the president replied for him, quietly mumbling, "Because he forgot."

"Marcus!" Frederick exclaimed.

By that point, I didn't know what else to say. My own father had forgotten about my life and didn't even have the courage to think back to his past. So, I took a big sip of wine, hoping that I was a lightweight, and prayed for this night to come to an end.

Frederick proceeded to laugh awkwardly, only to say, "Well... This night didn't turn out the way I expected it to."

I drained my glass and started pouring more. A monstrous bulk of anger was flooding my nerves, never to stop. To calm myself, I started thinking about Boney and everyone else, hoping that they weren't found and sent back to the prison. After all, I bet they were the whole reason I was sent into this dining room in the first place. If the guards were to find them, I'd probably be as good as dead. I doubt my father wanted to keep me around.

After finishing my second glass, one of the waiters replaced the empty bottle. I guess I wasn't a lightweight because I was barely intoxicated.

"Calm down, Charles. Just relax now and enjoy what you have," Frederick urged.

"For now," I replied.

"What do you mean by that?"

"I know what you're doing here, Frederick. All you want from me is a list of names."

"What names? Son, what are you talking about?" He replied.

"The prisoners who've escaped. After I give you their names, I'll be as good as dead to you. And don't call me 'son'. I know you don't see me as your son."

This was pure repetition. People always need something from you. And once they've obtained what they need, they get rid of you.

"That isn't true," Frederick said. "None of what you just said is true. You know that."

"Oh, but it is," I replied in a somewhat drunken voice.

Frederick's mind was being devoured by my constant babbling. He knew that I wasn't a fool, and I thought the same of him. As I started to think once again about my friends from the caves, another idea barged into my mind.

I thought, *Was my father actually the king of this city? From how he's acting around Frederick, it looks like Marcus is just a messenger.*

So, I asked my father, "Are you the owner of this palace?"

"That question came out of nowhere..." Frederick replied. "Although you seem kind of drunk, so I guess I'm not too surprised."

"Are you? Just answer the question."

"Uhm... Yes, why do you think I'm the head of the table?"

"Because it's your birthday."

Frederick laughed. "That's a fair guess." Then he leaned in closer to me and said, "And just so you know, Charles, I'd never let anyone take this seat from me; not without a fight."

I chugged another glass of wine and continued, "So, then… Are you the real president of this city?"

Frederick glanced at Marcus and replied, "I guess you can say that. After all, I'm the one who built this city from the ground up."

"But I thought—"

I was cut off by Marcus, "I just pose as the people's leader. Frederick didn't want attention to be thrown on him, so I take the duty of making people think I rule. But in reality, I'm just the messenger… It's a great job. The pay's getting my kids through college."

"I still don't see the royalty in any of you dogs," I replied, letting the conversation fade away in my memory.

An hour had passed, and I stopped drinking because we ran out of wine. While I was talking with Frederick, Aria sat alone in silence; she was barely eating. Eventually, I joined her.

As the dessert started to come out of the kitchen, Marcus asked, "You were late for dinner. What were you doing?"

"I had to deal with a lawsuit. The entire thing is completely ridiculous, but what can I do?" Frederick replied. "Some psychic is trying to take us to court. The trial takes place in a town or two over. I was baffled by how they found this address," Frederick continued.

"Yes, that sounds annoying," Marcus said.

"It is, but I'm sure my lawyer will find a way to work it out."

Dinner finally concluded. It was now around eight o'clock; the best time for loitering in front of the fireplace as it had begun to rain outside. All the guests fled into a beautiful room filled with furniture and a large painting of a boar which hung on the wall. I could hear a loud wave of chatter running through the hallways and rain crashing onto the grass in the background. For a brief moment, the setting seemed quite peaceful; I felt like all of my problems were slowly disappearing, except for my lingering stress about the others. Had I ditched them in the middle of a crisis?

"Sorry, but I have to check on something," I said.

"Where are you going?" Marcus asked.

"Probably to find his friends," My father said. "What are their names again? Let's see… there's the Annabelle woman and her father, along with another tall, muscular boy. Am I correct?"

Suddenly, my heart sank.

"How do you—"

Frederick cut me off, "I have my sources, Charles."

15

"I want an actual answer," I said. "How do you—"

Again, Frederick cut me off and said, "Somebody gave me this information, if you could guess who it was."

I was thinking and I couldn't really come up with anyone. I looked over at Aria and she was also clueless as to who would have told Frederick anything. Then I thought deeper and finally, my senses got to me. It must have been Victor.

"Victor," I replied.

"You're right. Good job," Frederick replied. "He really was a desperate man, selling out his peers for another chance at life."

Frederick stood up and walked across the room. He reached for a lever that was embedded into the wall, using it to open a hatch on the floor that revealed a dark cage. Suddenly, I saw Boney, Miss Annabelle, and Griff in a prison that lay under my feet. It seemed that my father had been able to locate them in a matter of two hours.

"I found these three walking around by the side of the palace," Frederick said.

"Frederick, give me the key," I replied. "Once I leave with my friends, we won't have to see each other again for the rest of our lives. I promise… I won't ever show up here again."

Frederick had a disgusting smile on his face, thinking that my words were some kind of joke.

I stood up and Frederick sat down, crossing his legs, and looking at the painting on the wall in front of us.

"Now why would I release these prisoners?" Frederick asked.

On the wall beside us, I saw a set of swords, which were probably used as decorations. I didn't think they were sharp, but they did look intimidating. The handles were made of gold, like half of the other things here, and I assumed that the swords were made with actual steel. I took one of them off the wall and pointed it at Frederick's neck. I didn't know if I was committing a pointless robbery of Frederick's time, or an actual attempt at an escape.

"Give me the key," I demanded.

The tip of the sword was practically touching his skin.

"Not a chance," he replied. "They're prisoners, Charles. We don't want scum like them walking free in our beloved city."

"I swear to God I'll take this sword and slide it straight through your neck," I threatened. "Give me the key."

Frederick wasn't moving an inch because he knew that I wouldn't kill him. It was clear that I despised him for all the hell he'd brought on me my entire life, but even so, I didn't have it in me to commit such an immoral crime. However, I had to seem threatening if I wanted to get anywhere, so I continued moving the blade closer to his neck and began to slide it across his skin. A tiny river of blood began to move down his shoulder into his jacket. *The tiniest cut always delivers the most pain,* I thought. *That should be enough for me to negotiate.*

I could see Frederick think and think, hesitating to move.

"All right, I'll make a deal with you," he said. "I typically don't do these sorts of things, but since you're my son, I'll make an exception."

I was immediately intrigued, even though a torrent of anger overtook each and every one of my other thoughts.

"Go on," I demanded.

"I'll let you live inside the palace, and I'll let you pick one of your friends to stay with you, but the others will all be executed," Frederick said. "What do you say?"

I didn't mind the offer except for the fact that two of my closest friends would have to die, so I came up with a lie.

"Fine, now give me the key to unlock the cell door and I'll decide who can live and who'll die."

Frederick most likely thought I was bluffing. In fact, he probably knew I was bluffing. Nonetheless, he handed me the key which had been in his pocket all along.

"Thank you," I said.

"You're welcome. Now leave and decide who lives, while I stop this bleeding," he replied.

I walked out of the room as Aria came along and shut the door, leaving my father to enjoy his peace and quiet for a short while. Then I locked the door from the outside.

It was finally time to begin our search. The palace itself was unbelievably spacious, each room leading to another. We traveled through the hallways, wondering where we were going until we reached the dining hall once again. On the side of the dining hall, we eventually found an old wooden door which was covered in a row of locks.

"Could that be a basement?" Aria asked.

"I don't think so; a basement that belongs to my father would have more locks," I replied. "That's probably a tool storage or something."

Aria didn't seem to think I was correct, but at that moment, we didn't really seem to care since time was scarce. Eventually, we covered the entire bottom floor and finally stumbled upon a door that seemed to lead to the basement. I opened it and found a tunnel made of old gray bricks making up the walls with a series of torches leading the way. I took the first step into the tunnel, and after jogging down the darkened steps, we reached the bottom. Immediately, I could see a line of cells along the back wall of the basement.

"God. This place looks grimmer than death itself," Aria stated.

As her echoes flew around us, I couldn't agree more with what she had said. The cracks in the walls looked like skulls. A forest of disgusting mold, along with a collection of strange weeds, grew out of the corners of the room.

After walking around for a few minutes, we stumbled upon the cell where Boney, Miss Annabelle, and Griff sat. It wasn't very large, and I knew that Frederick was watching us; he was memorizing my every move.

"Charles!" Boney exclaimed. "What's going on?"

"How is it possible for you three to get trapped like this?" I asked.

"I wish I knew. Somehow the guards knew that we had escaped the prison and then ran us into this dungeon, saying that we would all be hanged," Miss Annabelle explained.

"I see," I replied while kneeling to Boney's height. "I want to be blunt with all of you."

"What do you mean by that, Charles?" Boney asked.

I exhaled. "I know it sounds odd, but it turns out that my father runs this place. The entire city. He was the one who locked you three in this cage."

"Your father?" Griff asked. He was clearly confused and so was everyone else.

"I know, it sounds odd. Just go with it. We don't have a lot of time."

After the three in the cage grew silent, I continued, "Long story short, my father offered to let only one of you live. He plans on hanging—"

"Hanging?" Miss Annabelle exclaimed. "Charles, are you serious? We've all been friends for years! Now you're telling me that you're going to let your father—"

"Look," I said, cutting her off. "I know this sounds bad, but—"

Griff butted in and said, "Are you really going to do this to us? You haven't even seen your father in what? Three years now? But suddenly, he comes back into your life and now you're going to bow down to him like he's some sort of almighty king?"

I touched the bars of the cell and leaned in closer, just so that when I whispered, the authorities couldn't hear what I was saying. I looked back and the door was still shut; the dungeon remained desolate.

"Look. We're going to escape tonight and leave this city once and for all," I whispered. "We'll go somewhere far away. I promise. I never trusted my father and I never will. I'll never bow down to him like his guards and I'll never let him kill you three."

A pause of silence ensued while everyone looked at each other. We were all still somewhat frightened and confused about the situation at hand.

"How are we supposed to escape from this cell?" Boney whispered back.

I reached into my pocket as Aria watched my back, hoping that the dungeon was still empty. I took out a rusty silver key which looked older than universe itself and waved it in front of their eyes. I was careful not to snap the fragile key when I injected it into the slot. Once I rotated it to the right, I heard a loud click and the door to the cell opened, creaking and rattling. Suddenly, after everyone walked out of the cage, the door fell over, causing a loud crash against the floor.

"Now that I think about it, we probably could've knocked the cell door down by ourselves," Miss Annabelle remarked.

Without another moment to lose, Aria grabbed my arm and said, "Quickly, let's go before Frederick gets out. We probably don't have much time left," trying to lead us up the staircase.

As we rushed up the long path of stairs, something came into Griff's mind.

"So, your father's name is Frederick?" Griff asked.

Curiosity never can fade away from existence. Along with Aria, I explained everything to Griff, Boney, and Miss Annabelle. I explained how my father was an irrational tyrant, how Marcus wasn't really the president of this city, and I went deeper into the deal I had made with my father. Obviously, I cheated him, so escape was now our only possible option.

After running back up the stairwell and finally exiting the basement, I looked around the palace and the guests there seemed to flee off into their rooms. As I searched the main hallway, I noticed I was getting sidetracked because leaving all this wealth felt like such a shame. But what else could I do? I didn't want my past to catch up with me and cause the death of my friends.

When I returned to the door that led into the stairwell, I saw that Boney had stumbled upon the room covered in locks that I'd found earlier.

"Boney," I said. "We're about to head out. Let's go."

"No... Not yet," He replied. "There's something about this room... it's enchanting."

"What are you talking about?"

"I want to see what's inside."

What? Is he insane? I thought.

"That room's probably a tool shed or something like that. It's insignificant. Now come on, we don't have a lot of time."

He muttered "no," and stared at the door.

Seriously... What the hell is going on with him?

I looked back and nobody else wanted to move until Boney was out of the door first. He was the most fragile of us and if he was to die, another part of each of our souls would die along with him.

"Boney, we can't get sidetracked. We have to leave before Frederick finds us down here," I exclaimed.

Boney ignored my remark and asked, "Do you know where I could find a pair of pliers around here?"

"Dad, what's come over you?" Miss Annabelle asked him.

Griff grabbed Boney by his waist and pulled him back. Boney struggled as Griff started to worry; the apprehensive look on his face explained his feelings.

"Griff, do you know what's wrong?" I asked.

Griff knew what was happening and I saw the difficulty in his face. Nevertheless, he wasn't a doctor, so the certainty of his predictions wasn't entirely reliable.

"I remember my granddad having dementia," Griff said. "He'd also have random outbursts like this. One time he'd gotten angry at a tree because he thought it took his couch, so he stood outside for twenty minutes, punching at it until my dad brought him back inside. At the time, we couldn't explain what was wrong with him, but after a visit to the doctor's office about a year later, we'd finally learned the truth."

"You think that's what this is? Dementia?"

"Maybe. Maybe not... I'm not a doctor so I'm not too sure."

I noticed the deadly look in Boney's eyes. His hair was whiter than snow and sooner or later, it would decay.

As my conversation with Griff came to an end, Boney suddenly turned vicious, forcing Griff's rock-hard back against the locked door. Due to Griff's unbelievable strength, the door collapsed. After witnessing Boney's temporary phase of insanity, if it was at all temporary, I became worried that Boney was indeed sick.

The door was now on the ground, laying there without further cause. A stairwell was leading down somewhere but I couldn't see where it went. All I could see was darkness after the sixth step. So, in accordance with Boney's sudden desire, I was the first one to go down. As I stepped onto the first stone slab, I heard a frightening echo come up from the bottom of the stairwell. The second step was even more frightening, and as I made my way to the sixth step, the demons I couldn't see were calling my name and welcoming me into their cave. The others were standing back, waiting for me to reach the unseen bottom. Boney, on the other hand, was excited to explore the chamber. So, once I hit the seventh slab, Boney was the first out of everybody else to enter the stairwell.

Boney was now walking slower as he calmed himself down. The stairs grew darker and gloomier but as we reached the end of the stairwell, I stumbled upon a chamber. Inside, I found a wine cellar with an incredible number of bottles covering the walls. Each bottle was covered in dust and the walls were covered in mold, just like the basement. A couple of torches were spread out through the cellar, lighting up the wine racks amid pure darkness. The fire from the torches couldn't reflect off the bottles of wine because there was no glass that was visible. All anyone could see was dust.

"This is ridiculous. They're going to find us," Miss Annabelle complained. "And what's the point of having all those locks on that one door if there's only wine in here?"

She's right, I thought. *This room doesn't look too special. Why would it need to have so much protection?*

As everyone else was talking, I could hear their words from across the room. Their echoes traveled further than I thought, quickly bouncing off the walls. I strolled through the chamber and nothing interesting came into sight except for a small sparkle that came from one of the wine bottles. I was in the back corner of the cellar when that little speck of light blinded my left eye. So, I followed the light and eventually discovered a clean bottle of wine sitting on one of the racks.

What's this? I wondered. I thought my mind was deceiving me.

I reached for the bottle, and it was in fact clean. It had a clearly drawn marking on it that looked familiar: a cluster of strange symbols that were also on the torches in the prison.

This symbol… Why do I keep seeing it everywhere? I thought. *What is my dad's obsession with these symbols?*

Then I whispered to myself, "Should I taste it?"

From a distance, Miss Annabelle exclaimed, "Did you say something, Charles?"

"Nope!"

I doubt anybody will notice, I thought. *So, why not?*

Eventually, I removed the cork and a few hundred glowing diamonds suddenly flooded out of the bottle.

16

I examined a handful of stones from the bottle, and they appeared to be of high quality.

"Hey, look at this!" I yelled.

I flipped the bottle over and diamonds were pouring out. As the others crowded around in the back corner of the chamber, their attention was caught by a glimmering stack of wealth which piled high on the grimy floor. Every diamond looked uniquely different, each one being more expensive than an entire roasted pig.

"Wow... they're beautiful," Miss Annabelle marveled. "But all of this seems off."

"It does," Griff agreed. "Do you think every bottle in this room is filled with this many diamonds?"

"Let's find out," Boney replied.

Boney took another bottle off a shelf which caused a wave of dust to fly through the chamber. As Boney studied the bottle, twisting and turning it in never-ending circles, I noticed a strange amount of light coming from the inside. I took the bottle from Boney and smashed it against the ground, spilling another pile of diamonds onto the floor.

"Well how about that?" Griff exclaimed.

I strolled over to one of the shelves, closer to the center of the chamber, when I stumbled upon another bottle. This one had a red stamp on the front which was the same red stamp I'd seen a million times inside the prison. I was wondering if this bottle was anything special.

At this point, I wasn't sure if we were exploring the chamber or robbing it of its valuable reputation. Whatever the case was, I didn't care because of what my father did to me, so I opened the bottle and a sudden, strong scent escaped. This time, the scent of a bitter wine filled the air.

What? That's odd... I thought.

I walked past the other shelves and grabbed a glass before blowing off the dust. The glass felt scratchy, but I didn't really have a problem with that. As I went in for a taste, Aria walked over; she found me slouching against the wall.

"This wine isn't too bad," I said. "Want a glass?"

"Sure," she replied.

I poured her a glass, but after emptying out a majority of the bottle, I saw something floating inside. I was curious and grossed out at the same time, but amid that, I carefully tilted the bottle so that it wouldn't spill out the rest of the wine. The image of my curiosity grew larger as I kept manipulating the bottle. As it turned out, a piece of plastic-wrapped paper, about the size of my hand or maybe even larger, was inside. The paper was all ripped and tightly forced together by a rope which was barely visible to the naked eye.

After realizing that a piece of paper was floating inside the glass, Aria and I put our glasses on the floor, along with the bottle.

"Is there anything written on it?" she asked, bending over to see what I'd found.

The paper was difficult to unfold, mostly because the knot in the rope was tiny and my nails were too long to deal with it. But after fiddling around with the knot for a few minutes, we were finally able to untie it. As the roll of paper unfurled, a wall of tiny words flushed my eyes. At the bottom, I saw the signature: *Gloria Jamison.*

"Who's Gloria Jamison?" Aria asked.

Her? I thought. *Doesn't she work in the prison? What's a debt collector's name doing in a bottle of wine in my father's house?*

"She's a woman I remember from prison," I replied.

As Aria was about to speak, I heard footsteps come from the top of the stairwell. Frederick walked into the cellar and closed the door behind him. He was clearly looking for me and the others; perhaps he wanted to kill us. However, he couldn't see us; I was certain of that. The darkness of the cellar made us invisible.

From the distance, I heard one of my father's guards say, "Sir, are you sure you want to go in alone?"

"Yes," He replied. "Now shut up and wait upstairs."

"But…"

He was now yelling, "Do what I say! This is my mistake, so I'll deal with it myself!"

An awkward silence followed, only for the guard to turn around and command his subordinates to follow suit.

After seeing his face, I stood up and grabbed Aria's arm, running into the maze of shelves behind us.

"Charles?" Frederick exclaimed; he sounded ferocious. "Dammit, son. Where are you?"

Frederick's voice made me jump. I hushed and so did Aria as we watched Frederick pass by. I could hear each of his footsteps which were slowly circling throughout the room.

Soon, Frederick walked past the half-empty bottle of wine which I'd left on the floor. He seemed to notice the specific red stamp on its surface. When he bent over to pick it up, I saw the fear in his eyes burst into the air, causing him to spill the rest of the wine onto the floor.

Now terrified, he exclaimed, "This isn't funny, Charles! Where did you put it?"

It was now obvious that Frederick was looking to retrieve the piece of paper I'd discovered. I couldn't read what it said because there wasn't a shred of light around me, but I knew it was important.

I walked along the pitch-black walls as Frederick walked next to a torch, fully revealing himself to us. I couldn't seem to find Griff or any of my other friends, but even so, I realized that my father couldn't do anything; he didn't have any guards to protect him. We could have easily ganged up on Frederick, but instead of turning to violence, I felt like following Frederick in the shadows, knowing that he couldn't find me.

After playing a strange round of hide and seek for the next two or so minutes, I saw Frederick stumble into the bottles we'd broken earleir near the back of the cellar. He kneeled down and grabbed a handful of diamonds, observing the damage done. At that moment, I stumbled out of the shadows, hoping that Griff would spot me, so I'd have some sort of assured protection. I stepped onto the visible part of the stone floor which caused an echo to fly through the air. Without hesitating, Frederick turned around and saw me standing there. I saw nothing but anger spreading throughout his body, now abiding through the air around him.

I said, "I'm impressed... It only took you eight minutes to get out of your office. I wish it had been that easy to escape your prison."

After taking a step towards Fredrick, I unfolded the piece of paper which had Mrs. Jamison's name on it and waved it in front of his eyes.

"So, you were able to find my vault," Frederick said.

"It's incredible that you've collected all of this over the years," I said. "Especially those diamonds."

"Listen to me, Charles—"

"The miners... Is this where all their hard work ends up? In your vault?"

Frederick looked at me with hatred, thinking that I was still too immature to have a serious conversation. Maybe I was, and to show that I was even more of a child, I threw another bottle off a nearby shelf. I could hear the glass abruptly break, causing another flood of diamonds to travel across the floor.

"It's a business, Charles," Frederick replied. "The miners find diamonds for me, and in return, I give them shelter."

"Yes, and that shelter is a prison."

Frederick walked past me and opened a hidden hatch which was connected to the wall. Inside, there was a conveyor belt, transferring diamonds directly from the prison to his chamber.

"How else would I be able to pay for this city?" He continued.

I had now realized that my father was not a true business owner; he was a bottom feeder, grabbing assets from other people's hard work for his own enjoyment. He was a disgrace to me and this entire city.

"So how is Mrs. Jamison involved with this?" I asked, taking yet another bottle off his shelf.

Threatening to break his bottles was my best chance at intimidating him, so I always made sure to have one in my hand.

I continued, "Why is her name on this paper?"

Then I took the note and forced my eyes onto the writing, seeing the name Mrs. Jamison written out in script.

"She collects diamonds, gold, and other goods from the miners and sends them my way," Frederick said.

I looked at the paper as a river of sweat started to run down Frederick's forehead.

By that point, Griff had snuck out of the shadows; I saw him behind Frederick, slowly advancing on him.

The top few words written on the paper were:

Anyone of the Jamison name who holds this deed has full control of the palace under any jurisdiction. Shared ownership is not allowed. The original owner of this deed is: Gloria Jamison, however upon her absence, the youngest member of the Balkin name is immediately given precedence to take temporary ownership.

Under Mrs. Jamison's name, there was the familiar red stamp from the caves.

After rolling the paper back up, I realized just how annoyed I was with my father. He had lied to me; he wasn't the owner of this palace, nor this city. He was nothing more than a figurehead at one point who had taken the place of Mrs. Jamison. Frederick had sent her into the caves and used her as his own personal bank.

"Charles, give that back to me right now!" Frederick exclaimed. "That document is for the eyes of a true leader, not scum like you!"

Without another moment to lose, Griff jumped out of the shadowy abyss and trapped my father in his arms.

"Wait..." I mumbled. "This means Mrs. Jamison owns this palace and this city."

He exhaled and replied, "That's a mere technicality."

"This doesn't seem like a mere technicality."

"Charles, just let me go—"

I cut Frederick off and said, "Shut up."

Frederick was still struggling to the point where he became red. I folded the piece of paper and put it into a small pocket which branched off my jacket.

"Let me go. I'm the proud owner of this city!" he screeched. "Let me go! Guards! Help me!"

Lightning was now roaring through the air, and I was at the peak of control. Boney and Miss Annabelle, along with Aria, ended their period of hiding and proudly stood in front of Frederick.

We left the palace with Frederick. I was standing outside with Griff as the others rested inside the fortress. All the guards rested inside while the rain fell all, now afraid of me because of my newfound ownership over the city.

"What are you fools doing?" Frederick yelled. "Guards, lock him up! Stop ignoring me! All he did was show you an old piece of paper!"

His clothes were ripped up and covered in mud; he had nothing left. Frederick was on his knees. A bunch of tears rolled down his face; they were running with the rain, representing the sorrow of this very moment and the rest of his life in exile.

"They won't listen to you anymore," I said.

Frederick continued to struggle while Griff carried Frederick to the front gate as it slowly opened.

"You can't just kick me out!" Frederick screamed. "That's not how any of this works! You can't just take a piece of paper and claim that everything here belongs to you!"

I looked at the deed and replied, "According to this, it says I can."

Despite the rain, a crowd of people gathered at the gate to watch Frederick cry.

"Enjoy retirement, Dad," I mocked.

I knew I was being harsh, but I was also speaking for the oppressed; the people who had been forced into the prison, and the people who were forced to mine for the sake of my father's wealth.

"I'm your father. Stop this!" he yelled. "Guards! Do something!"

Griff threw Frederick past the gate and into the mud. He rolled over as the gates began to close, leaping up and trying to run back to the palace. But of course, it was too late; he was now the fool, and I was the ruler. The crowd on the other side of the gate remained silent as Griff and I strolled back into the palace through the rain. Marcus would be next.

17

Ever since the day Frederick left the city, rain had been showering the ground. Hundreds of people had lived inside the palace before Frederick left, and I let all of them stay because I didn't know what else to do with them. The authorities listened to me wholeheartedly because of the strangely recent power I had over the palace and the city itself. I'd always kept the deed in my front pocket, guarded by a wall of sturdy material and a zipper just in case something should happen.

Boney's room was adjacent to mine, and it was in the very center of the palace. He was so close I could hear his coughing every night before bed. As the days passed, he seemed to be getting sicker. One night I was sleeping when I was suddenly awoken by Boney, who was whispering to somebody through the walls.

What could this be about? I thought.

I connected my ear to the wall between our rooms and heard him mumbling something.

"Daddy Light, you're dead, like a ghost, like beautiful red blood…" Boney whispered.

What the hell?

Eventually, I walked out of my room, dressed in nothing but my robe to investigate. As I walked over to Boney's room, I noticed that the palace looked grim and dull in the moonlight; everything felt so empty, even with the hundred or so guests that took up the other rooms.

I walked closer to Boney's door, and the whispering seemed to grow louder. Boney's insanity was getting to me. I opened the door ever so slightly which caused an ear-breaking creaking sound to break out. Nonetheless, Boney continued with his episode of insanity. I looked through the crack to find Boney staring at the corner of the room, tapping his finger against the wall and whispering strange things to himself.

"Please Daddy Light…" he continued. "Save me from this place."

Now disturbed, I closed the door and went back to my room. Going back to sleep was difficult because I began to worry about the old man.

Might as well have a glass of water while I'm up, I thought.

I made my way down to the kitchen and a few chefs were already busy preparing breakfast. The light in the kitchen was blinding as my eyes adjusted. One of the chefs greeted me but the others ignored me until I accidentally bumped into one. Things became clearer as my eyes adapted to the light.

The chef I bumped into was wearing a giant white hat and an even whiter robe which was able to stretch onto the floor like the roots of a tree pushing through the ground. The chef was angry, mostly because I had spilled some of the red jam he was preparing onto the floor. I realized that the spill burned a part of my leg which stung for a second or two, but then it went away.

I apologized to the chef by saying, "Sorry about that."

But the chef seemed to ignore my apology. Instead of resorting to peace, he grabbed a knife from out of nowhere and put it to my neck. Then he complained, "What the hell are you doing?"

I was flustered.

"Goddamn… Don't worry, I can clean this up," I said while stepping back.

The man frowned at me.

"Hurry up before they bury you in the Greensburg cemetery," the chef demanded.

I had suddenly grown curious. "Greensburg? What is that?" I asked.

The chef looked at me and could tell I'd just moved here. I hadn't explored this city and yet, I was considered the king of it, even though nobody really knew about my rule in the first place. Frederick had known everything about the area from corner to corner, which made me seem like a fool, but I was planning to explore it sometime soon, even though I had been procrastinating for the past couple of days.

"How can somebody be so clueless?" The chef declared. "This is Greensburg. You're standing in it, you idiot. Are you new here or something?"

Oh, so that's the name of this city! I thought. *It's funny to think that I was technically the leader of a city whose name I didn't even know.*

Funny enough, the chef taught me more than my father had in the past few years. I appreciated that for a second or so, but now I had to rise to the other problem: his spilled jam. I gestured for the chef to put down the knife, but he refused, so I had to be more vocal.

"You should put the knife down," I urged.

"Not until you clean up this mess."

I glanced at the corner of the kitchen where I saw one of *my* guards, impressed that day and night, people were willing to protect their new president. It was possible the authorities might have despised Frederick's earlier rule, so I figured I had a well-rounded chance to show off as a new leader.

I called the guard who had been standing in the corner; he was not paying attention to anything in the first place.

He ran over to me and asked, "Yes, sir?"

Suddenly, the guard noticed the knife near my neck and leapt to my rescue. Within those few seconds, he knocked the weapon out of the enraged chef's hand and threw him to the ground.

"What the hell are you doing?" the chef yelled, struggling in the guard's grasp.

The infuriated chef's face grew scarlet.

"If you couldn't tell, I'm your new boss," I said. "I'm the one person in this whole city who you shouldn't be pointing a knife at."

The chef's face didn't change. I thought he might have been too shocked for the shift in his emotion or maybe he was too impolite to apologize.

"Clean the mess!" He yelled.

A group of guards ran into the room upon hearing the commotion.

"Clean it yourself!" I commanded. "After all, I'm the one who's paying you."

The chef's face reddened even more. Suddenly, he grabbed another knife from his back pocket and knocked the guard off of him. He lunged at me and tossed the knife in his right hand. Without thinking, I dropped myself to the floor and the knife flew past me, hitting one of the guards to my right. As I turned around, I saw the wounded man fall to his knees, collapsing right in front of me and forming a lifeless shell.

Oh my god... I thought. *What the hell is wrong with this guy?*

One of the other guards took out his gun and tilted it against the chef's forehead.

"Shoot me, you clueless—"

And the chef was cut off by his death. The bang from the gun echoed through the walls of the once silent palace and began a large commotion. People were woken up and started to fill the hallways. One of the guards knelt down and removed the knife from the fallen guard's neck. When he turned it over, he noticed that there was a small piece of paper stuck to the back of the blade.

"What's that?" I asked.

The guard replied, "I don't know, sir," and gave me the paper.

I unraveled it and found a letter written on the inside.

What is this? I thought.

I began to read it aloud.

Dear Charles,

You've taken over my beloved city, and yet you're a mockery. My riot will soon end your rule and I will be there to watch.

Yours truly,

Dad

<u>18</u>

The note was burned with every other document my father had owned. I got rid of Frederick's personal records and whatever else I could find in his old office. It had been two months since the chef's attempt to kill me; up until now, my ruling seemed to be going well. But one day, I heard a strange noise coming from the front gate of the palace. It was the middle of the day when I went outside to find a big riot taking place outside the gate. When I looked into the crowd, I guessed that there were around one hundred people protesting. Some were throwing torches through the gate, trying to set fire to the front lawn. Others were merely shouting swears.

One of the men in the crowd yelled, "There he is! There's the idiot who ran our *real* president out!"

"Kill him! Kill him you useless guards! Kill him!" somebody else exclaimed.

There wasn't only an uprising for the sake of my execution but there was now some sort of dispute between the townspeople themselves. It looked like I had some supporters in the crowd as well.

"Go to hell!" somebody shouted. "He knows what he's doing!"

Griff, who was standing to my left, said, "I'm guessing this is your father's work."

I exhaled and replied, "Looks like it."

As I watched the two groups dispute, tension seemed to be rising. Before long, a fight broke out involving everyone. I saw anarchy starting inside the city and sooner or later, it had the potential to break out. Miss Annabelle, who was watching the fight as well, was standing to my right, inhaling the damp fog that had surrounded us.

"What did I do to make them fight like this?" I asked.

She was unsure of an answer, so Miss Annabelle replied, "I wouldn't worry. I bet this will all go away after some time."

As I was talking with her, blood started to fly from people's fists and screams arose from outside the gate. At this point, I had wished the gate could grow ten times thicker, knowing that there was only a single piece of metal guarding the palace from devastation. Half of the demonstration tried to break down the gate while the other half was fighting with my supporters.

"Should I call the guards? One of them told me that most of them are playing poker in the palace basement. They're probably going to be angry," I muttered under my breath.

"I think that's all you can do," Miss Annabelle replied.

And that's what I did. I called the guards, disturbing their poker break, which caused them to complain more than I'd ever heard. Nonetheless, they followed my orders. Guards came in multiple waves, and they wouldn't stop flooding the front gate until the unrest broke loose. After ten minutes of hysteria, the riot ended with a series of men and women being arrested and sent to a local jail.

After the altercation was over, a few puddles of blood were splattered against the front gate and burnt sticks littered the ground. As a line of my guards stood at the palace gate, trying to clean up the aftermath of the riot, someone ran toward the palace with a binder full of papers hanging off his shoulder.

"Charles, Charles!" The man yelled.

What now? I thought.

Two of my guards knocked the apparent trespasser to the ground and held him by the arms and legs, taking him through the gate as it closed behind him.

"What is it?" I said.

The man was out of breath and took a moment to calm himself. He was quite short and had messy hair, like that of a tribal savage.

"Pardon me Ch... I mean, sir. But you were... you..."

"I missed what you're trying to say," I muttered, tired from everything that had just taken place.

The messenger continued, "I have a note for you, given to me by somebody in Salem Village."

"Who in Salem Village?" I asked.

"I don't really know, but—"

I cut him off and demanded, "Just give me the envelope and go rest."

Within seconds, the authorities whisked the man away and took the envelope right out of his hands. The unique design on the envelope interested me but not as much as the stamp which sealed the front; it was the same ruby red design I had seen mark the prisoners in the caves.

I ripped open the envelope and retrieved its contents. I unraveled multiple pieces of paper and looked at the first page.

Dear Charles Balkin,

It has come to my attention that Frederick Balkin was discarded as the president of Greensburg. Since you are the president now, you must deal with certain responsibilities in your city, along with a few outlying areas. Firstly, please note that, in some sense, Greensburg is a "secret city" in

Massachusetts. It isn't shown on any maps and isn't talked about very much because Greensburg is formally considered a company; a diamond collection company to be exact. Even though we have citizens who live here, you can consider them as just employees. I thought you might want to be informed about this.

Anyway, we've had a recent case open up where Frederick was accused of burning down a psychic's shop and you have now been asked to be a member of the jury. I was able to pull some strings with the judge to get you on the jury, regardless of the corresponding legality issues, since Salem Village is... also run by a friend of mine. Although Frederick doesn't know that, and it's better that he doesn't.

In short, you are expected in "court" by April 25th at noon. It's best that you don't ask any questions. All you need to know is that we need him gone for a while, so your first job as ruler is to play along with everything and be a good juror.

And just to warn you: if you decide to skip the court date, I'll personally come back up to the surface and shove twenty of my finest brass bullets down your throat. Good luck!

Sincerely,

Mrs. Gloria Jamison

19

It was the next morning when a carriage and two beautiful horses stood in front of the palace. A man with a mustache which was longer than Griff's thick, yet scrumptious feet sat behind the steeds.

Our driver greeted me, Miss Annabelle, Griff, Boney, and Aria, "Well, it's not every day I get to encounter royalty."

I replied, "Uhm... Thanks."

The driver started laughing.

"My name's Mr. Gliss," the man announced.

After the rather awkward interaction, I took a step into the carriage, along with the others. The carriage itself had a solid top but it was open on the sides with a railing made of wood; overall, it didn't seem very sturdy.

Once we'd taken off, I whispered "Why the hell are we taking a carriage to the courthouse? Where's our car?" into Griff's ear.

He replied, "Oh, stop complaining. It's a nice day; enjoy the weather."

"Aren't we going to be late to the trial?"

"No. Salem Village is close by. Stop worrying."

I huffed and looked at the surroundings. Griff was correct; the flowers and trees along the way were all quite beautiful as the water from yesterday's light drizzling sparkled on the greens.

After gazing into the distance for a while, I knew that we were now leaving Greensburg. To get out of the city, Griff said the carriage would have to pass an almost insignificant hidden valley bordering the bay of a large lake, which described our exact location.

"When do you think we'll get there?" Aria asked, uncomfortably shifting in her hard seat.

I could see why she didn't like the seats. They were made of damp wood and were poorly supported by the few dry sticks.

"I'd guess… about an hour or so," Mr. Gliss replied.

I nodded and then glanced at Boney; he looked worse than ever, scratching his forehead, and continuously whispering strange nonsense to himself. His feet were on the bench, and he was rocking back and forth like a lost seahorse.

"Boney, are you okay?" Griff asked.

Griff seemed to be more frightened of Boney than anyone else in the carriage. On the other hand, Miss Annabelle didn't really seem to care about Boney's unsettling attitude. Out of all of us, I would have expected Miss Annabelle to be the most paranoid about her father.

We were now outside of Greensburg, about half an hour away from the palace. The ride itself wasn't very entertaining and the driver was quiet. Miss Annabelle was reading a book which didn't seem to have a visible title on the cover and Boney was whispering something to himself which I personally couldn't understand. Griff and Aria were looking outside while I stared into my lap.

Suddenly, we stopped moving. I heard an unexpected crash as the horses started knocking their hooves against the ground.

"Hey, what's going on?" I asked.

The driver jumped out of the carriage and ran around to the front.

"We there yet?" Griff mumbled, waking up from a short nap.

Mr. Gliss scratched the top of his forehead and replied, "It looks like we've got a break here."

I looked over at the front of the carriage where a single wheel had broken off and snapped in two. That also caused a small crack along the edge of the rim to expand which meant that the entire thing would soon break apart.

"How'd this happen?" Griff asked.

"Not sure," Gliss said. "Guess we've gotta walk from here on."

"What about the horses?" Aria considered.

I looked back and saw the horses circling around the broken-down carriage. The driver followed them, trying to get closer, when they suddenly ran off into the distance.

"Hey! Get back here!" Gliss yelled, trying to make chase but soon stopped, realizing that the idea of catching them was unlikely. Then he continued, "Get back here! I feed you and shelter you for three years and this is how you repay me? You damned brats!"

"Come on," Griff said. "I'll carry Boney on my back."

And so, we were off. We began walking in the center of a grassy field during what felt like the largest heat wave I had ever experienced. My legs were already begging me to quit. We weren't following any sort of road but just over yonder hill stood Salem Village.

As the sun moved down, we separated into smaller groups, having our own conversations as we walked. Miss Annabelle was talking with Boney, and Griff had paired up with the driver. I was having a quiet conversation with Aria about this trial we needed to attend. She first complained about why she and everyone else needed to come, seeing that I was the only one who was invited. I told her that I needed people by my side, especially Griff, just in case someone who was tied back to my father tried to attack me.

"The trial Frederick mentioned earlier, do you recall what it's about?" I asked. "I know it has something to do with a psychic and him burning down her house, but that's it. I remember him talking about the whole thing during our dinner together in the palace, but I can't seem to recall any of the specifics."

"God knows what happens in that town," Aria replied. "Just forget about it before the glitter of it all kills you."

All my attention was suddenly taken by Griff who yelled, "Hey! I see a cabin just on the border of the lake!"

Aria replied. "We should stop by. Maybe we can get directions."

"What's wrong with my directions?" Mr. Gliss asked.

I added, "Asking for directions every once in a while doesn't hurt anybody."

Gliss pouted and seemed upset at first but complaining clearly wouldn't help anyone at this point. So, as we made our way closer to the lake, we were able to clearly view the facade of the cabin and its traits. The door was halfway destroyed, and the windows were made with ripped nets. The pungent scent that surrounded us resembled a mix of muddy water and rotting fish that had been sitting out in the heat for weeks. Overall, the cabin looked forsaken; it had an uncomfortable vibe to it, and I was sure that everyone else agreed.

"Well, who's going to walk up these steps and knock?" Mr. Gliss challenged.

His question was followed by silence. After waiting for the entirety of a minute, I was getting impatient.

"I guess I'll do it," I said, walking in front of the others.

Let's hope whoever lives here isn't some kind of sociopathic killer. I thought. *Because that's all that I'm getting from this house.*

I took the first step up the stairs and as my foot combined with the wood, a loud creaking sound emerged from the board. It seemed so contradictory that such a creepy cabin was resting beside such a lovely lake.

"Come on, Charles," Boney prodded. "You're walking up those stairs as if the owner of this house is going to jump out and stab you in the neck. Hurry up."

I hadn't forgotten about Boney's sickness; his brain was turning darker, and his personality was growing different. He had turned into a rude, impatient old man who always seemed to whisper to himself.

"You'd do the same if you…"

Boney made me shut up as he ran up all three of the steps and stood at the front door. He was now taking over the situation.

Is he not at all apprehensive? I thought.

Boney started banging against the wooden frame and yelled, "Hello? Anyone home who'd give us directions to Salem Village?"

"My God. Calm down," Miss Annabelle said.

Suddenly, I could hear footsteps marching from the inside of the cabin. By now, I was nervous to see who'd come out. The doorknob started to turn, and the door opened very slowly as Boney stepped back, motioning me to walk up the steps and stand beside him. I could see an eye pop out of the darkness from inside of the cabin.

"What do you want?" the man demanded in a somewhat scratchy voice.

"Sorry to disturb you, but do you happen to have directions to Salem Village?" I asked.

I tried my best to be brief.

"Sure… Come in," He replied, swinging the door wide open. "Just make sure to close the door behind you. I don't want flies getting in."

When the door flew open, I could see the old man in front of me. The others creeped up the steps after I entered the cabin first, making sure that nothing suspicious was waiting for us inside. Even though I confirmed that the cabin was safe, I admitted that the inside looked even creepier than I thought it would. The walls were covered with rusty fishing rods hanging out of cut-off animal heads that were mounted on the walls. The tables were moldy, and clumps of strange green weeds were growing out of the cracks in the structure. As for the cabin owner, it was obvious that he didn't look as old as Boney, but he also wasn't very far behind. He had a white beard which extended to the sides of his head and a scar which rested above his left eye. His overall appearance was like Boney's, except he'd never heard of hygiene before.

The old man began to pour water into a glass, but when I saw the actual water, I was disgusted; it was the color of wet sand, even though we were far from any ocean.

"So, why are you all going to Salem Village?" The old man asked.

"Jury duty," I replied.

"Oh, that doesn't sound like a lot of fun."

Once the final glass of water was filled, the old man closed the window beside me. Seconds later, everything around me had fallen into darkness. The room quickly became black because my eyes had fallen asleep.

20

For a split second, I couldn't feel anything. A deep headache was slowly consuming my head while the others came to their senses. Things were slowly growing clearer; I was tied to a wall, meters away from Griff who still seemed to be in a trance. The old man who had knocked us out was nowhere to be seen. I was the first to awaken, looking at everyone else who seemed to enjoy their sleep. As my eyes readjusted to the dim light within the cabin, the old man walked into the room; he was holding a rusty can that was filled with a pungent substance. He was whistling and humming, minding himself to what was doing.

As I continued to look around the room, I saw a calendar on the wall with the days marked. It was April the 24th and the legal case was due on the 25th. Suddenly, I realized my predicament and thought, *Court is at noon tomorrow. If I'm stuck here for the rest of today and the night, I'll be screwed!*

"Hey! What the hell do you think you're doing?" I said.

The old man jumped and turned around, looking me in the eyes. He replied, "Wow, you woke up faster than I expected."

I was getting increasingly irritated, and my voice showed that. "Just tell me what you want, old man!"

"Don't call me that; I'll let you call me Jotsy."

"Alright, Jotsy…" I replied, now ready to beat the old man through a brick wall. "What do you want from us?"

"Well… I've always wanted my own horse, bred in Italy, and brought here overseas. Maybe a fine—"

I cut him off and retorted, "I have something important to do! Stop joking around; what do you want from me?"

His face suddenly grew stealthier. "Oh, well I saw you and that old man next to you on a wanted poster back near Greensburg, and I want that reward those men are offering."

"What? A wanted poster?"

"Yeah. When I visited there a few weeks ago, I saw a bunch of them hanging near the outskirts of the city."

After hearing him speak, I realized that this was the inner workings of the riot that surrounded my palace a few days prior; they were tracking me down, hoping to kill me for Frederick's sake.

"So, he's trying to get the deed back..." I mumbled to myself. "If it comes to it, I might have to kill Frederick."

"Frederick? Who's that? That name sounds familiar," Jotsy asked, now pouring himself a cup of water.

"He's the president... No, the former president of Greensburg," I replied.

Jotsy seemed confused. I didn't understand what there was to think about, but he went against all simple beliefs.

As our conversation passed, Jotsy seemed to look for something near the lamp which lit up the room. He messed with some of the papers on top of the kitchen counter and observed them. It seemed to be a newspaper.

"My god, look at that," Jotsy said.

"What is it?" I asked.

"Well, apparently this Frederick guy you're talking about has been dead since yesterday. It looks like the dead are even coming after you."

Without thinking, I didn't believe him. Even though I'd robbed Frederick of his home, I knew he was a powerful man. He was just too powerful to be dead.

"Where'd you get that newspaper?" I asked.

"Some guy stops by the cabin on his way to Salem Village every couple of days and offers me a copy of the paper."

I sighed. "Let me see."

Jotsy turned around and showed me the front page of the newspaper. It mentioned that a "Frederick Johnson" died after an oak tree fell on him in front of the local bank. Unfortunately, that tree fell on top of the wrong Frederick.

The day went on as Jotsy started to move a few of his things from the main room to a small storage room in the back of the cabin.

"So, who's in charge of this riot thing you've been mumbling about?" Jotsy asked.

I couldn't think of anyone who despised me as much as my father, so it was most likely him, however for the time being, I wanted to act like I wasn't sure of anything.

"Don't worry about it," I replied.

Then Jotsy scrambled through something in his room. When he entered the main room again, he was carrying a large fishing pole which was about as tall as Griff. As he set it down against the front door, he grabbed a tattered sun hat for himself.

"Well, if any of you need me, I'll be back in an hour or two. I have to catch tonight's dinner," Jotsy said, opening the door to leave all of us stranded.

"Alright, but what if—"

I wasn't able to finish my question as the door shut; Jotsy was out of sight. When I looked away from the door, I noticed that Griff started smiling—he was finally awake.

"How much of that did you hear?" I asked.

"Doesn't matter," he replied. Griff started to struggle and demanded, "Charles, can you reach that half-broken pair of scissors on the table over there?"

I followed Griff's finger and said, "Uhm… I'll try."

There was an old marble table next to me which was adjacent to one of the windows. Everybody's hands were trapped behind their backs, and it was the same with our feet, hogtied to the wall. I was impressed that Jotsy was able to do all of this in the time I was asleep.

Speaking of sleeping, what did Jotsy use to knock me out? I thought.

I would have guessed that raw fish was the answer, seeing that was all he had aside from random slabs of wood. Or it could have been some kind of drug he'd planted inside of that sandy water, although I didn't see any pill bottles anywhere in the room.

"Can you see it?" Griff continued.

"Yes."

I kept bumping into the table, hoping the broken scissor would be able to fall off and avoid my skull. After rocking back and forth for a good five minutes, I eventually heard something drop. It was the scissor.

"Oh, I can't believe that actually worked!" Mr. Gliss exclaimed from out of nowhere.

Since I thought Mr. Gliss was asleep, I jumped and hit my head against the table. Griff seemed to take the compliment more than I did.

As my pain went away, I reached for the scissor by biting it with my teeth like a horse taking a carrot from a farmer's hand. I was then able to place it in Griff's hands, leading him to cut the rope which hogtied his feet to the wall. Griff's hands were strong enough to break the rope around them, which is why I'd given him the scissors first. After freeing himself from the grasp of the old man's trap, he cut my arms free and I was able to cut him in turn, along with my feet. After freeing ourselves, the two of us cut everyone else free and we were in good enough condition, except for Boney, to flee the cabin. Of course, we still had to wait until everyone else woke up.

Twenty minutes had passed as I was the first one to run out of the cabin, hoping that Jotsy or the people who were hunting me wouldn't see us. But as we left the cabin, it seemed that luck had turned against me. As I gazed out at the field in front of the cabin, something in the distance suddenly caught our attention. A mob of people holding torches and pitchforks were walking along the pathway to the cabin. They were heading directly towards us.

"Do you think they're from Greensburg, Charles?" Aria panicked.

"Maybe," I replied.

We began to run but remained close to the cabin since we still had to arrive in Salem Village. The hill we were hiding behind was close to the lake, about fifty feet away, so if the riot passed the cabin, I could hear their conversation and see it as well.

The sun was starting to set as Jotsy met up with the riot at his front door. I could clearly see some of them in plain sight. One man who wasn't holding any weapons walked up to Jotsy and raised his chest. The man was trying to seem superior even though he didn't have a say in anything unless the others in the group agreed.

"Hello, Tommy Gensin," the man said.

Tommy? Is that Jotsy's real name? I thought. *Why would he lie to us about his name?*

"Hello, Bobby," Jotsy mocked.

"Acquaintances refer to me as Mr. Alexson. You got that?"

Jotsy seemed to understand and looked too afraid to retort.

"So, where's that criminal you promised you'd catch?" Bobby continued. "Charles Balkin?"

"I caught him this morning. He's inside this cabin now," Jotsy replied meekly. "He brought a few of his friends with him, too."

However, when he opened the door, a collective gasp of annoyance and betrayal came from the riot. It was clear that nobody was inside of the cabin.

"Tommy Gensin, I don't see that Charles boy in here. Now stop playing around and tell me where he's at, or else I'll do what I promised you over the phone," Alexson threatened.

Jotsy was silent; he couldn't respond with anything helpful because he was still shocked that we'd escaped. It was clear that the riot was growing impatient, and I couldn't help him. I was the cause of his imminent demise.

The riot leader replied to Jotsy's silence by saying, "I see."

"I'm sorry, sir," He eventually said. "I caught them… I swear I did."

Alexson walked around the front of the cabin and grasped Jotsy's shoulder. He said, "Do you know what I do with liars, old man?"

With a quiet and nervous voice, Jotsy mumbled, "Please, Mr. Alexson..."

He chuckled at Jotsy's anxiousness and commanded the riot to throw a flock of torches at the lonely cabin which once seemed to be in a peaceful rest.

"No! Please sir, don't do this to me! I'll get anything else you want, sir, I promise!" Jotsy begged.

"Shut up!" Alexson remarked as he kicked Jotsy in his ribs, causing him to fall to his knees.

"Stop! Stop it, you monsters!" Jotsy exclaimed.

Suddenly, Jotsy grabbed his fishing pole and vehemently sliced at Bobby's knee. In the course of Jotsy's desperate assault, I was able to spot the intensely large mark now all the way down Bobby's leg to the very top of his foot. Blood started seeping from the mark as other members of the riot started to cover the streaming blood with a few old rags.

"Wow... That escalated quickly," Boney whispered.

"It really did," Aria added. "It's mutiny."

"Shh, something's about to happen," Mr. Gliss whispered.

In response to Jotsy's attack, Bobby snapped his fishing pole in half, throwing it into the burning cabin. Then he grabbed somebody's pitchfork and stared at Jotsy. The tyrant started to scrape the tips of the pitchfork against Jotsy's skin without showing a drop of mercy. Jotsy's screams were painful to hear. Bobby had forced the tip of the pitchfork down Jotsy's stomach three times, rolled him over and then started with his back. The astonishing part was that other members of the riot seemed to enjoy all of this. The agonizing screaming seemed to be music to their ears. Those three scratch marks which ran down his body looked like some strange satanic symbols I'd see in the devil's book. The blood which flew through the air was dark red, as red as a beetroot or, in my mind, the surface of Mars. At this point, Jotsy looked like a pie, his skin being the dough and everything else being the cherry filling.

"They're monsters…" I whispered to my friends.

Jotsy was now lying on the ground. Blood was leaking from him like a burst dam. At this point, he was as good as dead.

21

The moon was barely glimmering that night. All I could see was darkness, besides the flames which were burning Jotsy's cabin into nothingness. Salem Village was still a good distance away and avoiding my father's riot was making our lives much more difficult. I was surprised that the insurrections were still going as violent as they were.

"That was horrible," Aria mentioned.

"That was worse than horrible," Mr. Gliss added.

Mr. Gliss didn't know about the prison, at least to my knowledge. Torture and hostility were two words I would have used to describe that place, and Bobby Alexson had displayed both of these traits to the extreme. I'd already seen events like this one occur on my way to the mines, so I wasn't very shocked at the entirety of it all, but I *was* astonished by the fact that something like this would occur on the surface.

While everyone tried to move past the show that had just occurred, Griff pointed north and yelled, "Look over there!"

Up ahead, there was a fluorescent light being emitted from the darkness. However, I couldn't see what was causing it because of the hill over yonder.

"What could it be?" I asked.

"I'd guess Salem Village. One of my cousin's told me they've got beautiful lights," Mr. Gliss said.

This was the light I missed and envied for such a long time. Back in the prison, everyone wished they could lay in a grassy field in front of the Moon and look at the lights in the night sky. If it weren't for the caves and my father's cruelty, I could have relaxed in the grass and watched the lights until morning. But that was only a dream.

As we made it to the top of the largest hill in the field, Salem Village became visible. Lights were shining through the wind and not a single flame was in sight. I could see the courthouse; it was wooden and taller than the towers rising up from Greensburg. The courthouse had wooden pillars in front of it and the Massachusetts state flag waving back and forth in front of them.

"Do you think we'll be safe here?" Miss Annabelle asked.

"Probably not," I wondered aloud.

We entered the village the next morning to find crowds walking the streets. The market seemed to be filled with goods I hadn't seen in Greensburg before. A fire pit sat in the center of the market, where a couple of people sat around, singing songs which were also unfamiliar to me. It was soon to be noon, which meant court would begin within two hours.

The clock was minutes before eleven as Mr. Gliss directed us past the courthouse. This made Miss Annabelle ask, "Wait, why are we passing the courthouse? Aren't we supposed to wait there?"

"Everyone in this town knows that during church hours, the courthouse is closed," he replied.

"What?" Griff said. "That doesn't seem legal..."

He chuckled and replied, "It is in this town."

Mr. Gliss rounded us up around the front door of the church where crowds of parishioners were waiting for the doors to open. Sunday was an exciting day for the people of Salem Village and for the first time in ages, I didn't mind taking part in church. I also found it somewhat strange that court was being held at eleven in the morning instead of noon. As I continued to think about our situation, I quickly realized that everything about this town made little to no sense. Between Greensburg's existence, the court being closed during church, and the hailstorm which had just occurred at Jotsy's now blackened cabin, I had trouble differentiating imagination from reality.

The stroke of eleven eventually rang and the doors flew open, not a second too soon. The bishop welcomed me in, along with everyone else. I took a seat on the freezing bench which was surprisingly much more comfortable than the carriage that had taken me halfway here. A podium was standing at the center of the stage for the priest who wore a long-white robe. He walked to the front of the congregation and waited until the room grew silent. A few children wouldn't stop crying in the back as millions of small glittery particles and dust floated through the air. But once the children were either taken outside or shushed, the priest cleared his throat and held up a Bible which looked older than the church building itself.

"Good day, my beloved brethren. As we all know, today is the anticipated murder trial between two of our own residents. May we pray for our beloved Frederick and Sabrina?" Father said.

Aria leaned over to me and whispered, "So your father lives here too?"

I didn't have the energy to come up with a reply, so I nodded at her.

"I give my sincerest gratitude to any of our own who have to partake in these unfortunate grievances," the priest continued.

I didn't think Frederick would attempt to murder someone. He never really seemed to be violent or murderous on his own. Usually, his guards would be the ones to do his bidding, but now that they no longer work for him, he would be all on his own. I started to think about him some more. Did I commit a crime in stealing his home? After all, I had snatched the deed to the palace and the city illegally. Although, after reading Mrs. Jamison's letter, it didn't seem like she cared. Perhaps I was overthinking things.

Anyhow, after praying, Father started to discuss all of the problems with the courthouse that he wanted to cover, although the details were generally minor. At least, I think they were minor... I zoned out during that entire discussion. I was too busy thinking about the fact that this church session was more of a town meeting than anything else. While the priest mentioned the bible a few times, most of the meeting seemed to revolve around civil issues, like the issues with the courthouse or a faulty intersection by the edge of the town.

As the day goes by, this town's only getting weirder and weirder...

Once the hour of discussion and praise came to an end, the church session officially concluded, and the courthouse doors swung open. The entire town rushed across the street and lined up, waiting to take over the courthouse like a hoard of hogs running into a barn. Of course, I followed suit.

As I crossed the street and jogged up the courthouse steps with my friends at my side, I blinked and accidentally walked into a lady. She was wearing a pink dress which looked old, but it did a wonderful job at bringing out the two giant dimples on her cheeks.

"Sorry," I said.

"Oh, I should be the one saying sorry. I'm clumsy," she replied.

I wanted to make some sort of conversation, feeling somewhat uncomfortable to abandon such an awkward interaction.

"So, why are you watching this case?" I asked.

"Oh… well, things like this don't happen much in our town," she laughed.

There was silence once again.

"My name's Allison… Allison Von Hildia, just in case you'd wanna talk again," she offered.

"Oh, yeah. I'll see you around. I'm Charles. I gotta get going before the other members of the jury are annoyed that I'm late," I said.

"You're part of the jury? That's incredible! And for such an important trial too!" Allison exclaimed.

"Thank you," I said, walking into the courtroom.

We waved goodbye to each other.

When I walked inside, the bailiff recognized me and let me onto the jury stand. As I took my seat, I realized that the case was more serious than I'd first thought. My own father was riding the line between freedom and prison, and his fate would be entirely within my grasp. I didn't think that all of this could be possible, yet I was somehow there. Perhaps I was never registered as Frederick's son in any actual document. Or is Mrs. Jamison really that powerful? Could she pull the judge's strings in a way that would inevitably get me on the jury? I suppose a better question to ask is: why me? Out of everyone else, why does she want me to put my father away for good? And why would she want to get rid of him in the first place? There were so many questions revolving around in my head all at once, although it was clear that I wouldn't be getting answers from her anytime soon.

Minutes after the courthouse doors flew open, the courtroom became packed; there was not one chair left in the audience. On the right side of the stage, everyone could see the defendant: Frederick Balkin, with his lawyer who looked colder than the top of the mountainside. On the left, everyone could see Mr. Gliss's brother, Jays, who Mr. Gliss had told us about before the church session. He was tall and had a peach face; I could see his well-rounded resemblance to Mr. Gliss. I could also see Jays's parents who seemed to be more stone-faced than his lawyer. Frederick seemed to have a few people behind him in the front row, but I couldn't figure out who those people were. In fact, they were both asleep.

The judge entered the courtroom as everyone found their seats. I was in the back section of the jury and Frederick hadn't noticed me just yet. The judge's gavel was forced upon his table and called for everyone to rise.

"You may be seated," the judge said.

Then he shuffled through a stack of papers which were most likely documents concerning Frederick's past.

"This is the attempted murder case of Sabrina Smith, going against Frederick Simpson Balkin," the judge exclaimed. "The plaintiff may now begin with his opening statement."

Jays's lawyer rose and made his way to the center of the courtroom. As the judge turned his head to the left, now facing the plaintiff, Jays's lawyer started, "Good afternoon, your honor."

22

Jays was sitting inside of the witness stand, waiting for questions to smother the courtroom left and right. He seemed to look average in my opinion; he had brown curly hair, eyes which were shining in the light of the courtroom, and a typical black suit. The judge looked through a series of papers which were spread over his desk until the hour fell quiet. Jays's lawyer was in the center of the courtroom, holding his hands behind his back and waiting to speak again. The judge finally piled the stack of papers together and shifted his attention to the lawyer who patiently waited for some desolate sign of beginning.

"Please rise," the judge demanded.

A bailiff walked past the jury holding a Bible. He was much different from the authorities in Greensburg. Here, the bailiffs wore sheriff hats which held a golden star in their center, and their light brown uniforms didn't match the black and shiny shoes which went along with their belts.

"Do each of you solemnly swear that you will fairly try the defendant which stands before you, and that you will return a true verdict according to the given evidence and instructions of the jury, so help you God?" the clerk asked.

In unison, the jury said, "I do."

The judge nodded and said, "You may now be seated."

I couldn't discuss matters with anyone in the jury except within my own mind, so nobody else could hear. I wanted to hide any evidence that Frederick was my father. It seemed that I was alone in this court case, lacking any jurisdiction over the defendants. The others were watching the case as Frederick was counting on his lawyer for full freedom. Or was he? Frederick always did things by himself. He'd been sued a few times since he was nineteen and, in a way, he'd always represented himself. I couldn't imagine why he needed someone else to carry him around, as if he was a mule with a rope around its muzzle.

Jays was waiting for questioning to begin. His lawyer walked up to the stand and leaned along the partition. The clerk was the closest one to the lawyer besides Jays who didn't seem to be fully awake.

Jays's lawyer wore a name tag which read "Mr. Jeremy Gonsins".

"Jays, do you have any relation to Mr. Frederick Balkin?" Gonsins asked.

"Yeah. I used to go fishing with him down by that lake past town... I think it's about a mile or so back."

"And when was the last time you went fishing with Mr. Balkin?"

Jays scratched the top of his head. At first glance, it was clear that Jays didn't seem to remember much of his past with Frederick.

"When we were kids, about a decade back," Jays said.

I didn't see how their childhoods pointed to the direction for being accused of murder, or at least attempted murder. Nonetheless, I continued to listen.

"When did you decide that Mr. Balkin attempted to kill Sabrina?" Gonsins asked.

"Well, about a month or so back; I saw Frederick light the *Sabrina the Psychic* office down the block on fire and—"

Frederick's lawyer shouted, "Objection! Your honor, that's a blatant lie."

The judge seemed to have an interest in Jays's mention of the local psychic's storefront.

155

"I'd like to keep listening," the judge said, demanding Frederick's lawyer to take a seat.

I was thinking about who I wanted to be seen as guilty as the commotion continued. Frederick now knew that I was in the jury box, mostly because he kept looking at me every now and then as the case went on. I had the advantage of manipulating him, seeing that I was part of the group of people who would ultimately decide his fate. It felt wrong that I wasn't sure if my own father should be found guilty or not. I could have given him a chance, possibly a trade: proving him not to be guilty if he ended his childish rioting against me.

"Anyways, when Sabrina held my hands, she said she had a vision of Frederick burning her place down in the future, and she was right," Jays said. "That was about a week before Frederick burned it down with her inside. She said she wasn't sure why Frederick would've wanted to do such a thing... But he did, and now we're here."

Gonsins looked at the jury and then back at Jays.

"And Sabrina... is she still alive?" Mr. Gonsins asked.

"She is," Jays nodded.

"So then why isn't she the accuser? Why are you here instead of her?"

"Because she's afraid to come up here herself. She's not looking for any trouble and she's too afraid of him to do anything." He pointed at Frederick and then continued, "So, I said that I'd do her the favor of suing."

Gonsins nodded his head and said, "Thank you, Jays."

The judge started to think after hearing some of the testimony leading up to the murder accusation. Then he stared at Frederick's lawyer for some time before actually calling him up for the refute.

After facing Frederick, the judge said, "The defendant may now speak."

Jays started back to his seat along with Mr. Gonsins but Frederick's lawyer stopped him from going on.

"I call Mr. Jays Gliss back to the stand," Frederick's lawyer implored, walking up to the witness stand.

I was able to see the lawyer's name tag, "Mr. Gregory Hovkins."

Jays walked back and took the stand once again while Mr. Hovkins stared into his eyes. The audience hoped for the best in this pending conversation.

"Mr. Jays Gliss, earlier you said that Frederick had something to do with the burning of Sabrina's psychic office, is that correct?" Hovkins probed.

"It is," Jays replied.

Frederick's lawyer had a serious look. He stood up straight like a tower and seemed to frighten Jays more in that manner.

"And you spoke with Sabrina after the burning of her shop, is that correct?" Hovkins asked.

"It is," Jays repeated.

"And why did you talk to her?"

"Because we're good friends. I wanted to catch up; she did too."

Hovkins paused to think, reflecting on the fact that Jays answered every question without thinking; he was almost like a machine.

"But you said, in quote, 'when she held my hands, she had a vision of Frederick burning her place down in the future'," Hovkins said. "It sounds like you went to her shop for a prediction, not to catch up."

Jays squinted his eyes and replied, "I wanted both."

"I see," Hovkins replied. "Why did you want a prediction?"

For a moment, Jays was frozen in thought. Mr. Gonsins stared at him from his seat and smiled because he was starting to break him.

"That's my business," Jays said.

"Jays," he said. "It's important that you tell us everything you know. After all, this is a serious situation."

In a much quieter voice, he replied, "That's my business, not yours."

The lawyer exhaled and started, "Jays, I don't think you realize how imp—"

Suddenly, Jays screamed, "That's my business and mine alone!" while slamming his fist against the witness stand. "What do you not understand you murderer-loving sheep?"

The crowd gasped as the jury started to quietly murmur. The people watching the case immediately gossiped to each other about the rebuttal. Mr. Gonsins didn't seem surprised, but I was intrigued by the outburst. I didn't think asking somebody about their predictions would turn out to be such a soft spot.

The judge grabbed his gavel and slammed it against the rim of his podium. Then he demanded, "Order! Order in the court!"

The crowd slowly grew silent, and their attention was shifted back to the earlier conversation. The judge looked down at Jays and said, "Mr. Jays Gliss, if you do not go along with the defendant's lawyer, you will be held in contempt of court."

Jays looked down, infuriated. Gonsins didn't seem to object, which probably led to Jays' anger.

"Sorry, your honor," Jays apologized, looking back up and staring into Mr. Hovkins's devilish eyes.

"I will not ask again, Mr. Jays Gliss. Why were you getting a fortune from Sabrina right before her shop burned down?" Hovkins asked.

Jays didn't have any patience with Frederick's lawyer. If I were Jays, I wouldn't have wanted to be interviewed by him either. I too saw the intimidating glare being emitted from the lawyer's eyes, which didn't seem to sooth anyone in the jury either.

"I was getting the fortune because…" Jays said.

"You're stalling, Jays. Why did you want the fortune?" Mr. Hovkins asked once again.

"I wanted the fortune because I…"

"Yes?"

There was another pause. Jays's fists were growing red.

"You should really answer him, Jays," the judge reminded him.

"I was getting a fortune because I saw Frederick scoping out Sabrina's place earlier that day. I wanted to know why he was there and what he was doing, so I told Sabrina about Frederick and asked for a fortune so I could learn more about him and what he might do in the future. After a reading, Sabrina described a man who looked exactly like Frederick burning her place down. Since her readings are never wrong, at least not to my knowledge, I knew she'd be in danger, so I decided to take matters into my own hands…"

"How so?" Hovkins asked.

Jays twiddled his thumbs in midst of anxiousness and confessed, "I was planning to shoot him right then and there with my shotgun and then drag his body down to the lake."

23

Jays' plans to protect Sabrina struck his lawyer quite gruesomely. Mr. Hovkins, on the other hand, could only grin. Now everyone knew the extent of Jays's anger, which would ultimately draw waves of attention from the audience and the jury.

The judge took his gavel and forced it upon the rim of his desk yelling, "Order, order in the court!"

This was more of a repetitive statement. The audience wasn't very compelled when it came to the judge's demands. The gavel didn't seem to have much power over anyone at this point. The entire town, except for the children and a sum of adults, were inside the courthouse. Many of the photographers outside were quick to take a picture at any possible cost to the court.

Over the course of ten or so orders the audience settled down. The room grew silent once again and the conversation between Jays and Mr. Hovkins continued.

"So that means you tried to assassinate Mr. Frederick Balkin, am I correct?" Hovkins asked.

Jays still didn't seem to have enough authority in calming himself. He had his fists clenched and his teeth shut tighter than a steel vault.

"No, I never got to it. By the time I left Sabrina's, he was already gone," he said, slowly eating up the insides of the audience's dignity for Jays. "I never even got close to my shotgun."

A few seconds of silence followed. Then, as the clock struck one, Hovkins straightened his back and decided to halt his seemingly successful line of questioning.

"Thank you, Jays. That's all for now," Hovkins said as he went back to Frederick and took a seat with ravishing pride.

The judge was silent for a second as the jury watched. He looked at Jays who'd been busy grieving next to his lawyer. There wasn't a single speck of aberration anyone had noticed about Frederick just yet. He seemed to be calm and respectful, but at the same time, he looked far beyond distant.

"Alright, Mr. Gonsins, you can go on," The judge remarked, setting the side of his head against his palm.

"Thank you, your honor," Gonsins went on, "I call the defendant, Mr. Frederick Balkin, to the stand."

Gonsins stood up and walked to the center of the courtroom where he crossed desolate pathways with my father. Frederick looked at me again and ignored Gonsins for a split second. There wasn't any sign of change in Frederick's face when his eyes were able to spot me, but on the other hand, who knew what he was able to think? No matter the situation, I could never seem to get a grasp on his thoughts.

As I looked down, forcing my eyes to scrutinize the court's decaying floorboards, Gonsins walked up to the witness stand. He was stale faced while he looked down at Frederick.

"Mr. Balkin, I looked into your work files last night and noticed something quite peculiar," Gonsins began.

Frederick replied in a mocking tone, "I'm listening."

Gonsins didn't seem to look at Frederick. In fact, he wasn't looking at anyone, neither the audience nor Frederick. The most interesting thing in his field of view was the folder in his hand.

"It states here in Section One Subsection Three of one of your past publicly known contracts: 'Owner of Greensburg Prison and

Greensburg Palace… original structure: twenty acres worth of mineshafts; abandoned in 1874; set for economic rise in Massachusetts'," Mr. Gonsins stated. "Does this mean you're the owner of a prison?"

Frederick needed a moment to think.

"Well, it's more of a business than anything else," Frederick claimed. "I wouldn't quite call it a prison."

Gonsins seemed interested. Whenever Frederick mentioned something about the prison or Greensburg, he would always take a quick glance at me as if I was an enemy. The reaction was almost unconscious.

"Business? What do you mean by that? Prisons only belong to the government, am I correct?" Gonsins asked.

Frederick looked the lawyer straight in the eyes.

"I think you're taking this out of context—" Frederick mumbled.

Gonsins placed his right hand onto the podium. "Why don't I turn this into a yes or no question?"

Frederick grew silent, so his lawyer exclaimed, "Your honor, this has nothing to do with the case at hand."

After a second of silence, the judge glanced at Gonsins and said, "Is there a point to all of this, Mr. Gonsins?"

"Yes, your honor. Of course, there is."

The judge turned to Hovkins and replied, "Then I'd like to hear the rest of what he has to say."

Gonsins smirked and looked Frederick in the eyes. "This is a yes or no question, Mr. Balkin. Do you own a business?"

"Yes," He replied. "Yes, I do."

"And do you own a prison?"

With great hesitation, Frederick replied, "Yes, but—"

"So, your business is running a prison?"

"In a sense, sure, but—"

"And are there people inside of this prison?"

"Yes..."

"And these people who are inside of the prison... Are they captives?"

"Yes... They are."

"And is this prison in the jurisdiction of the state?"

Frederick lied, "Yes."

The lawyer glared at Frederick. "Then why can't I find this prison on any Massachusetts map?"

"It's relatively new, so I guess nobody's had a chance to put it on one yet."

"Hmm... And what relation do you have to this prison? Are you the warden or an investor? And how is 'Greensburg Prison' your business? And why can't I find any information about this place? None of this makes a dime of sense to me," Gonsins said.

Many thoughts moved through the audience. It was obvious that Frederick was lying, both about the legality of the prison and his status.

Suddenly, Frederick asked, "What does this have to do with the trial itself? We're talking about attempted murder, not my job."

Frederick and Gonsins both looked at the judge.

"Let Mr. Gonsins go on with his statement, Mr. Balkin," the judge demanded.

"Yes, your honor," Frederick mumbled with growing anger in his voice.

By this point, the room was almost dead quiet.

"Now Mr. Balkin, just how many individuals do you suppose are held in this prison of yours?" Gonsins asked.

Frederick seemed to grow impatient with the line of questioning; it was quite repetitive and didn't seem to have a purpose. Gonsins seemed to be an elderly man but somehow obtained the energy to continue.

"I don't recall the exact number of inmates," Frederick replied.

"I see. And just how do you run the prison itself?"

Frederick couldn't reply.

"Seeing that your prison is located in an underground mountainous area, is it a possibility that you tried to create the scene of Hell for the prisoners you don't own authority over?" Gonsins exclaimed.

"Alright, now you're just making things up!" Frederick exclaimed. "Of course, I have authority over them!"

Up until that point, I never saw Frederick feel threatened by another man's words before. By the ferocity in his voice, it sounded to me like he was being attacked. Was the lawyer's ridicule really enough to make him lose his sense of composure?

After Frederick's abrupt remark, the court's audience grew as silent as an audience could be, letting the sound of dust particles colliding with the wall stand out.

"Do you want the prisoners to think of you as a ruler? As a god which would soon lead into being a cruel man? A man willing to kill, only so he could hide something for himself?" Gonsins exclaimed.

"Objection!" Hovkins yelled.

"Shut up," the judge exclaimed, wishing to see if Gonsins was making a logical statement.

Frederick jumped from his seat and yelled, "What you're trying to do here isn't realistic, whatsoever! First, you've got some idiot talking about a psychic who sees the future and now you're saying I'm pretending to be some kind of God? What are you people talking about? This isn't court! This is lunacy! This has to be some kind of dream, because I feel like I'm higher than a kite when I have to listen to everything going on here!"

The judge slammed his gavel against the table and exclaimed, "Calm down, Mr. Balkin! I'm sure you don't want to see another charge be added to your already growing list."

Tension in the courtroom was rising and the case suddenly grew worse for Frederick by the second. The judge let Gonsins keep his point clear and finish the questioning for now.

Mr. Hovkins now had the authority to question another witness. At this point, both sides of the court seemed on edge.

Hovkins stood and walked to the center of the courtroom. He turned around and took a folded piece of paper from the inside pocket of his suit. Then he slowly unfolded it, as if he were trying to assess the patience of the jury at the same time.

Eventually, Hovkins took out a pair of glasses and started to read. "I have a list of people who are acquaintances of Mr. Jays Gliss, except for one which is scribbled out. I would like to call Miss Allison Von Hildia to the stand."

"Objection! Your Honor, that's intrusion! That goes against my client's privacy!" Gonsins stated.

The judge sighed. "I'll allow it."

Allison slowly got out of her seat in the audience and struggled through a line of people to get into the aisle. She had been sitting in the middle of the second or third row which meant that she was visible to the judge's eyes ever since the start of the trial, along with that of the jury. She traveled past the steps which led her into the center of the courtroom as she made her way to the witness stand. Hovkins took a deep breath, then cleared his throat and turned around to where he could look the girl directly in the eyes.

Wait, that was the girl I'd met by the entrance of this place… She never mentioned her being a witness.

"Miss Von Hildia, is it true that before the beginning of this case, you were in direct contact with Mr. Jays Gliss?"

"It is," Allison replied.

"So then why did Jays scribble your name off of this list I have here?"

"I'm not sure," she replied. "Isn't that a question you should be asking Jays?"

The lawyer smiled and said, "No, not yet."

24

Allison wasn't very far from the jury; in fact, she was just a few feet away from me. If I didn't have the decency to reach my arm across the floor during the trial, I would have been able to touch her hand. Hovkins wasn't any further away from Allsion than the people of the jury as well.

Once the lawyer finished his previous statement, Allison paused for Jays to come up with a reaction. However, Jays expressed nothing; his face looked blank.

"Miss Von Hildia. In your honest opinion, do you think Jays is a child?" Hovkins asked.

Allison seemed relaxed. Her face was serene, even though the court case felt like it was spiraling into a void of confusion and chaos.

"Well… His muscles say otherwise, but I do admit that Jays tends to be childish if you compare him to the other people in this town."

"How so?" The lawyer asked.

"He's always really… Hmm, I can't seem to think of a good word."

"You can take your time, Miss Von Hildia."

After she thought for a moment, Allison said, "Rowdy. He's always so, so rowdy. Jays always makes a lot of accusations, like a toddler who doesn't trust anyone but his parents."

Jays glared at Allison; he looked like he was embarrassed.

"I see," the lawyer continued. "And in your opinion, do you think Jays' claims are logical?"

"How so?" She asked.

"I guess I should have been clearer. Do you think Jays is correctly accusing Frederick of attempted murder if his only evidence is a psychic reading?"

"Oh… I guess not."

The group started to murmur, although the judge didn't seem to care.

Allison continued, "But whatever's going on now feels different from Jays' other accusations. I mean… Sabrina's reading was correct. Her shop burned down, and the fire chief already proved that neither Sabrina nor Jays could've started the fire—"

Gonsins smiled and continued, "Allison, I'd like you to tell me something."

"Alright," She replied, almost flustered.

"Do you trust Jays?"

In response, she hesitated and said, "I'm not really sure how to answer… That's kind of a complicated question."

"Allison," he continued, leaning his right elbow on the rim of the witness stand. "It's a yes or no question."

"It's just that—"

"Please, just answer the question; we both know you're stalling. Now, let's try this again. Based on your past relationship with Jays, do you trust him? Yes or no?"

She stuttered and said, "No."

The lawyer walked closer to the jury and continued, "Miss Von Hildia, if you will, please tell the jury why you don't trust Jays Gliss."

"Sure," She replied, now sounding uncertain of herself, "But pardon my quiet voice. My throat is a little sore."

"That's no problem. You can take your time."

Hovkins' confidence was intriguing. He made it seem like Frederick was holding Jays in the grasp of his palms, even though he'd spent the past hour sitting still.

"About a year or two ago, we started dating. I'd met him on the bridge near the lake by the church, passing by to feed the doves when he stood there, throwing little crumbs onto the ground for the flock—"

"Did you enjoy your time with Jays?"

"Uhm… At first."

"Why 'at first'?"

"Because a few days later when I was supposed to meet Jays near the bar by Main Street, I saw him kissing another girl. At first, he tried to tell me the girl was his cousin, but I knew he was lying because the girl he was kissing was my cousin. Her name is Luna, and ever since that day, we haven't said one word to each other. What's funny is that she used to be my favorite cousin… I thought she was pure, because it seemed like she was, just by the way she'd act around me, or by the calm vibe that she would always give off. But I guess I was living in my own world…"

"And do you think Jays regretted his actions?"

She chuckled. "No, of course not. Even now, I see him walking around town with a new girl every two or three days."

"Really?"

"Yup," she replied, now glaring at Jays. "That's just the type of man he is."

"I see. Thank you, Miss Von Hildia. That's all for now."

As Hovkins walked away from the witness stand, Allison turned to Jays and mumbled, "And to think I loved you…"

Her voice sounded heavy, and as a result, I felt bad for her; we all did. Frederick's lawyer was doing a marvelous job at toying with our emotions. Slowly but surely, an infection of distrust and anger towards the plaintiff himself was spreading among the audience and the jurors.

Another few hours of discussion had passed when rain started to fall. It was visible through every window in the courtroom, along with the few strikes of lightning that hit the hillside. The church remained empty as it rested across the street with the court now in recess. "We will continue once the jury has made their decision," the judge announced. Then the audience rose, and a loud wave of chatter erupted as the judge walked out of the room. Jays quietly spoke with Mr. Gonsins and Frederick did the same with his lawyer. The clerk demanded that the jury retire to a separate room where discussion could proceed. I stood and felt a tingling throughout my legs. The case seemed like it had gone on all day. I saw Miss Annabelle talking with Boney who refused to stand as a few of the others were gossiping away.

Soon, the bailiff took us to the jury room in the back of the courthouse. To my surprise, it was quite large. The others took their seats and stared at each other until the clerk entered the room, taking a good look at us as he stood in the doorway.

"Attention, members of the jury."

The clerk was reading something given to him by the bailiff.

"This meeting will determine the defendant's fate: guilty or not guilty. You may take as long as needed; the vote must be unanimous. You all may now begin your discussion."

The clerk walked out and the only door out of the room clicked; it was locked from the outside, just like the Greensburg prison.

That's odd... They locked us inside? I thought to myself. *Oh well! After reading Mrs. Jamison's letter, I shouldn't be surprised about anything. Plus, this whole "court" thing that Mrs. Jamison set up, whatever it is, is probably rigged, anyway. In the end, this is all just one big act...*

I looked at each member of the jury and didn't seem to recognize anyone. A couple of the jury members lit a cigarette and slouched back in their chairs. One person threw his legs onto the table while another tilted his head back and closed his eyes. Silence was present, taking over the entirety of the room, and not one person volunteered to start the discussion.

Finally, a man with large glasses stood and started the conversation. He was the same man who put his feet on the table. "If you ask me, this trial is pretty one-sided, so I'm sure this discussion won't take very long."

I was silent.

Another man stood, "I agree, we should just vote that Frederick guy guilty and get on with our lives."

Since nobody wanted to reveal their name, I decided to nickname each person once they'd spoken. The first juror with the giant glasses would be Glasses, and the other juror with the giant hat and beard was Beardy.

Glasses stood once again.

"Wait! There's no way Frederick's guilty! This entire attempted murder case doesn't have a sense of realism. If Frederick wanted to kill Sabrina, he could have simply taken a knife and done the job; it would've only taken a minute. Plus, you can't accuse someone of attempted murder just because a psychic said that person was going to murder them!"

Suddenly, another man stood. His hair was curly enough to be a patch of vines and his head had almost touched the ceiling. I was referring to him in my mind as Curly. "To be honest, I agree. The defendant is innocent. We can't prove that he actually committed a crime. Besides, with of the girls he's manipulated and ghosted over the past few years, everyone in this town knows that Jays is a crook. He took my sister's innocence, and I'm sure that if you have a sister, he's taken her innocence too."

Glasses added, "I agree; Jays isn't making any sense here. A psychic reading isn't credible. And you're even more right about him being a prick; my cousin can confirm."

As I looked around the room, it was clear that Beardy was angry. So, with a treacherous voice, Beardy exclaimed, "You all may be right about him being a crook, but don't forget what Jays' lawyer mentioned." He coughed, muttered something to himself, and then continued, "Frederick was the only person to be seen around Sabrina's before the start of the fire for that entire day. Plus, if the fire marshal already proved that Jays and Sabrina couldn't have started the fire. He saw them at the central fountain when the fire started."

Beardy seemed to resemble Jays in a way; he was humorous yet insane. Beardy was always talking to himself whenever the others were in the middle of a conversation. He kept mentioning things about apples and how apples would one day kill us all. I had no clue what the man was going on about, so I tried to my best to ignore him.

Soon, another juror who was covered in clothes from the tip of his head to the bottom of his feet took a stand. He wore a suit, a scarf, large boots, and had a cane. I called him Scarf.

"I agree! It makes sense that Frederick is the killer here… I mean, look at the facts. He was the only one near Sabrina's. He was—"

"We don't have any evidence of that!" Curly interrupted. "These are all just accusations."

Scarf continued, "You may be right, but somebody burned the place down and nobody else has been named."

"I agree," I muttered, suddenly jumping out from my prolonged period of silence.

The rest of the jury shifted their attention to me, but I didn't know what else to say, so I sat back in my chair and let the others continue.

"Where's the proof that Frederick's a killer? Nobody saw him do anything!" Glasses exclaimed.

"None of you have a brain! Can't you people see? This Frederick guy had to burn down the psychic's shop. Nobody else could've done it! Everyone in this town knows each other. We're all familiar with each other in one way or another, except for that one 'prison tyrant' nobody who happened to walk into town right when this all went down. He's got to be the criminal here!" Beardy exclaimed.

"Why does any of that prison stuff even matter? This court case is about attempted murder!" Glasses exclaimed.

"What about the psychic? Her visions were correct," Curly mentioned. "Weren't they?"

Glasses said, "The only people who can vouch for her are Jays and herself. And where is this so-called psychic, anyway? How come nobody used her as a witness?"

"She's in a coma," Scarf replied. "She's been in one for over a week now. It's even in the newspaper."

A pause of silence pursued Scarf's statement.

I broke that silence by asking, "Should we take a five-minute break?"

"Yes," Beardy replied.

So, we sat in silence for the next few minutes, thinking about the case and its strangeness. I saw Beardy look through a pamphlet which rested on the top of a pile of papers in the middle of the table. Beardy seemed to read the pamphlet as if it was a book. For some reason, I could imagine a fishing rod in his palms like Jotsy, threatening to take the string and slice me to the bone.

Eventually, without my help, the jury had finally come to a decision. My vote was for Frederick to be guilty, as per Mrs. Jamison's orders. The other members of the jury also made their decisions and finally came to an agreement which took hours to discuss. We were sequestered for a total of four and a half hours, which was close to how long we'd spoken about the case in front of the judge. Court would soon end.

The other members of the jury walked back into the courtroom and took their seats. After a long day of discussion, everyone was thrilled to go home.

"Court is now back in session, please rise," the bailiff said.

The audience stood, along with the jury.

"Please be seated," the judge demanded as he entered the room.

The audience was on the edge of their seats as they awaited the verdict. The judge turned and looked past the clerk who was guarding the door and the jury members, specifically Glasses, who was supposed to announce Frederick's fate. I stood as hundreds of intimidating eyes were now looking at him.

"Your Honor, the jury has been discussing this case for quite some time now and we have come to the unanimous conclusion that the defendant, Frederick Simpson Balkin, is guilty of all charges," Glasses exclaimed.

As he sat back down, I thought to myself, *It's just like you wanted, Mrs. Jamison... And you didn't even need my help. I don't know how he did it, but Beardy somehow pulled everyone to his side.*

"Well, that does it. Frederick Simpson Balkin is guilty of all charges, and shall be sentenced to five years in prison without parole. Case dismissed," the judge exclaimed.

After the judge's final remark, he slammed his gavel against the rim of his desk twice, stood, and left his seat with the audience and the former jury following suit. As everyone scattered around the courtroom, Griff got up and walked over to me. He was about to say something when Frederick suddenly walked up to me. In a fit of rage, he said, "Charles, how could you vote me guilty? I haven't said anything for the whole trial, even though I noticed you in the jury box. I was depending on you to prove me innocent. I know you're still angry with me, but I'm your father, dammit!"

"The evidence proved you to be guilty," I replied. "I don't know what else to tell you."

"Since when did you care about evidence? I had Mrs. Jamison send you here because I thought you would be reasonable and help your father!"

"Wait, Mrs. Jamison said I would help you?" I replied. "That's not what she told me."

I turned around and started to walk away when he grasped my shoulder.

"Charles, what are you talking about?"

I chuckled. "She sent me here to get rid of you."

"Huh? What are you talking about?"

I pulled Mrs. Jamison's letter out of my jacket pocket and showed it to Frederick. After skimming it, his eyes widened. Then, as I put it away, I continued, "I guess her plan worked."

Frederick, now with a ferocious and desperate voice, replied, "Listen to me, Charles. I might seem like the bad guy right now, but you have to realize something. She's trying to get rid of me to take Greensburg and all of its diamonds for herself. I should have expected this, although I didn't think she'd try anything so soon."

I yawned and replied, "Okay, and?"

"What do you mean, 'and'? This is serious! You have to find a way to get me out of this, or else she'll take Greensburg for herself and kill you! Charles, you have to—"

In the middle of his sentence, I turned away and walked towards the front door. As I looked back at Frederick, I told him, "This is your problem. Maybe now you'll learn how terrible of an experience it is to spend your days wallowing away inside of a jail cell."

Without much left to lose, Frederick grabbed my shoulder and whispered, "I swear to you that I won't be stuck in prison, Charles. I have connections and when I'm out of this town alive, you'll go right back to those caves."

As I threw Frederick's hand off my shoulder, the judge saw me and waved me goodbye. I waved back.

Suddenly, Frederick took a knife from the back of his pocket and ran at the judge, quickly putting him in a headlock. As the bailiff ran over, Frederick brought the blade up to the judge's neck.

"Frederick, let go of him! He's just doing his job—" I yelled.

"You're a sin, Charles! How could you side with that cruel woman over your father?" Frederick exclaimed.

Since Frederick was focused on me, Griff was able to sneak up behind him and knock the knife out of his hand. Seconds later, Frederick was on the floor, sobbing his way into the grim world of isolation.

25

The next day came quickly. A bright morning sun forced all the folks of Salem Village to wander the streets while the children walked in a line by the side of the main road to get to school. I could smell the wonderful scent of bread cooling on somebody's windowsill and the freshness of a daisies consuming the grass around us.

"Doesn't that bread smell amazing?" Aria exclaimed.

"It does!" Griff replied. "Too bad I'm on a diet."

"What? Out of all people, why are you on a diet?"

He chuckled and flexed his left arm. "You don't get muscles like these by eating bread."

Boney nodded his head in disapproval and muttered, "That's fine by me."

"And why's that?" Griff asked.

"Because every time we eat together from now on, I'll be the one taking all of your bread for myself."

Everyone chuckled at the remark.

After walking down the main road, I looked at the distant mountain ranges and asked, "Miss Annabelle, when do you think the next carriage will arrive for our trip back to Greensburg?"

"Huh? Why would you want to go back?" She replied.

I squinted at her. "Why do you sound so surprised?"

"At this point, Greensburg's falling apart. The rioting for Frederick to regain leadership won't stop and I bet by now the palace itself is gone; for all we know, it's probably burned to the ground." After pausing, Mrs. Annabelle continued, "And for god's sake, I'm not your teacher. Call me Mary."

"Alright, Mary…"

I paused for a second and then attempted to answer her first question. "There are still some reasons to go back, at least temporarily."

She looked surprised. "Really? What reason is there to go back to that terrible place?"

"Well…" I mumbled. "We do have all those diamonds sitting in the vault. Plus, Aria needs to get back home. After all, her family lives in Greensburg."

Aria nodded. "He's right."

"Why don't you just stay with us, Aria?" Griff exclaimed. "I'm sure the people in this town would love to take us in as guests."

Aria replied, "I have family waiting for me back at the mountains. While I am flattered that you four want me to join you, I can't just leave my parents like that."

Griff mumbled, "I guess you're right."

"How about this?" I suggested. "I'll go back to Greensburg, get Aria home with her family, get some of the diamonds from the palace, and then come back here to Salem Village."

We stopped and thought about my proposition. Once the wind grew silent, Aria grasped my shoulder and smiled.

"I like that idea," Aria replied. "I'll also help you bring a few of your diamonds back to this town if you'd like."

Griff agreed and so did Boney, even though they seemed reluctant at first to let me go.

Finally, Griff walked forward and demanded, "I'll stay here with Boney and Mary. Don't take too long, or we'll get worried."

"Alright," I replied.

Then he continued, "And you might want to bring us back a few extra diamonds. The hotels here probably aren't cheap."

I laughed and grasped his shoulder. "Don't worry. I'll bring back as much as my pockets can hold."

Mr. Gliss didn't have his carriage anymore which meant that Aria and I belonged to a stranger. Instead of joining us, they decided to look for shelter in a hotel back by the church. The others didn't want to return to Greensburg either, even if they would receive a fortune for it.

After looking around for a while, we eventually found a man who was willing to hitch us a ride back to Greensburg. Later, when we passed what had been left of Jotsy's old cabin, Aria asked, "You think we'll make it past the valley without anyone noticing us?"

"Hopefully," I replied. "Let's just pray the city's still in one piece when we get back. If the guards did their job correctly like I told them to, we shouldn't have any problems."

That was when the carriage suddenly stopped. The driver jumped out of his seat and ran around the side. As he opened the gate to let us out, he said, "Well, this here's your stop."

"What? We're still over a mile away from Greensburg," I stated.

"Obviously, we're not there yet, but I'm not stopping anywhere near that Hell you'd call a home."

"Huh? Why not?"

"Cause every time I drive around here, I end up getting robbed of my money, my clothes, or even my carriage. I want to buy a car and make a taxi service, but they're so damn expensive and I am not making very much money by being robbed. So, good luck!"

Aria and I walked through the gate and the carriage driver quickly fled in the opposite direction at full speed.

When we walked past the valley, I could see the Greensburg I'd left behind. The palace was covered in mysterious stains and fires were burning in every corner of town. The air turned gray and the previous residents of Greensburg were long gone. Greensburg was now in the midst of anarchy.

26

My identity was hidden from the rioters; in fact, it was hiding in plain sight. The gate which used to block others from entering the palace were collapsed and the doors of the palace were broken down. I looked through one of the windows and saw several people sitting on the once beautiful furniture I'd kept in my office as a stampede of children tore down the restroom's wallpaper.

The first step I took back into the palace made me shiver because it was no different from the horrid past of my prison life. Afterwards, we made our way to the kitchen, which was filled to the brim with people I'd never seen before. About two hundred rioters drank from my once clean glasses which were filled with the wine from the bottles in the nearby shelves. The walls were covered in moss, or something that resembled it, and a million black spots which had the pungent scent of charred ash radiating from them. As I continued to look around, I saw a specific painting which hung on the center wall in the kitchen. It was the only one I could remember. There was a young woman who stood on top of a hill, holding an umbrella in the green, acidic rain. If I remember correctly that painting was made for my mother before her death.

I remembered coming home one day to see my father and a couple of guards standing on a ladder; they were tampering with the painting. My mother was touched when she saw it up close. I remembered walking through the arch in the kitchen doorway as Mother had picked me up. I believe I was about six at the time. My father climbed down the ladder to greet my mother, setting the guards to the task at hand. It might have been their anniversary.

That night at dinner, my father, mother and I were eating as a conversation came up.

My father lifted his fork and said, "I was able to kill off another one of those cheap businesses today before I got the painting."

Frederick owned a retail company, or something of the sort, which had a lot of rivals. He loved to sue different companies for numerous things which ended up shutting down too many rivals to count. I had never learned the specifics of Frederick's business or his tactics, but my mother used to tell me that his methods were making us richer; that's all I ever knew.

"Oh, honey, you should really stop with all this nonsense. Sooner or later this town's going to run out of stores, and we'll have to travel over to the next," my mother replied.

"Please. We'll be the ones selling everything; groceries, clocks, clothes, utensils, anything. You name it and it'll be on the list."

"Your things are expensive and this town's poor enough. They'll probably want to travel to get things for less at the market past the station."

"The train station?"

"That's the only station in this town."

My father didn't have much control, so whenever my mother would refute something of his, he would say something along the lines of, "Shut up! All of this is because of me. You hear? Not you. Me! And it'll *only* be from me!"

I took my eyes off the painting and looked around the room to spot the other changes within the palace. I thought about the authorities whom I'd deserted earlier and how they were most likely all gone.

When I turned away from the painting entirely, I saw a muscular man who wore a vest matching the color of his yellow teeth standing on the top of the kitchen table. He was shoeless and held a bottle of wine up with his left hand.

"My friends!" he exclaimed. "When that excuse for a ruler returns to this city from being a coward, he will be hanged by a new, stronger democracy!"

A wave of joyous screams quickly erupted. Aria and I pushed through the crowd as we walked past the kitchen into the open field behind the palace which also seemed to be filled with strangers.

"What happened here?" Aria said. "Everything's destroyed…"

"We should hurry up and get the diamonds before anyone recognizes us," I replied. "They probably haven't found them yet… At least, I hope so."

As we passed the crowds of people who brought the palace further into the ground, I heard a subject rise from a couple of distant conversations multiple times: a ball, a gala, a celebration. A ball in the middle of such a house would be unthinkable but I couldn't argue with anyone because I was the prey. I thought of myself as a steak for the lions in their cages; once I showed myself in Greensburg, I'd be slit more than a knife against a cutting board.

"Aria, what's this gala everyone's talking about?"

Aria looked surprised. "Do you not know what a gala is?"

"No?"

Once Aria made her remark, a nearby woman turned around and displayed her astonished face. She seemed to be tall, and her voice was deeper than ravine.

"You don't know what a gala is?" she asked loudly.

Once she asked her question, the voice spread to another person.

"You don't know what a gala is? Are you uncultured?" the other person asked.

"I was joking," I lied nervously. "We were just joking around… It's alright."

I kept listening in on the conversations and I ended up hearing that this gala was a celebration of my exile.

Eventually, once the crowd around us scattered, Aria whispered, "This place really has an ear for gossip."

"You don't say…"

Soon enough, we walked back into the palace. Then after loitering around for a bit, we walked into the ballroom while Aria explained what a gala was. My father had never taught me anything; I had simply enjoyed life through reading and sleeping.

When we walked inside, I noticed that the ballroom was the most crowded spot in the entire building. So, as chaos continued, we snuck through the ballroom and every other corridor which was packed to the brim with blood-hungry rebels. Eventually, we made it to the wine cellar door, ready to snatch our diamonds and run far away. However, as we walked closer to the entrance, it was clear that someone was sitting in front of the door, drinking whiskey straight from the bottle.

After seeing the man, Aria leaned over and whispered, "What do we do about him?"

"I don't know."

The drunkard was alone, wearing ragged clothes and old, dirty boots. Suddenly, another man joined him and asked for a swig of whatever he was drinking.

"You've got to be kidding me," Aria whispered.

"What?"

"There are two of them now."

I looked past Aria's shoulder and realized the increasing difficulty of the current issue. "What do you suppose we do?"

"What if… What if we pretend to be a part of the rioting and join in on the gala? They'll most likely leave when it starts."

My eyes widened.

"Are you kidding? They'd catch us within an hour! Plus, we're just here for the diamonds."

"Look… If we're careful, we should be fine. Plus, all we've got to do is be quick."

"It won't be that easy!"

"Everyone will be busy dancing and drinking. We should have enough time to slip away, retrieve a couple of diamonds, and leave before anyone would ever notice that we were here."

This isn't a bad idea… Or is it the worst idea that we've come up with yet?

Realizing that Aria's idea had been too risky, I nodded and replied, "No, we don't have enough time. Now come on, let's go."

"Go where?"

"What you just said is going to be our backup plan. Right now, we're going to try to convince those two to move."

"What? No! That's too dangerous. Somebody's going to—"

Without listening to the end of her sentence, I walked past the two drunkards and took a seat on the floor next to them. One of the men had hair running down to the floor and the other wore a pair of glasses and a belt which looked heavier than a block of iron. After he noticed me, the man in the glasses turned around and half-mumbled, "Hey, friend."

"Hey… Sorry to ask, but can you guys move?" I said. Then I pointed at Aria and continued, "We have to get a few things from the basement."

One of the drunkards suddenly looked up at me in confusion and anger.

"No! Nobody's allowed to enter," the man with steel boots announced.

"Why not?" I asked.

"Cause… uhm… that room's only for supplies and we can't afford any more of you pesky raccoons stealing our stuff…"

I looked over at Aria because I wasn't sure what to say. She looked annoyed, probably because I denounced her plan as our backup, so when I tried to reply to the man, she cut me off and said, "Can you idiots just move?"

"What'd you say you dumb broad?" one of the men challenged.

He started to stand but halfway up he slid against the wall and threw himself back onto the floor.

"Are you sure that was a good idea?" I whispered.

Aria ignored my whispers after hearing the two men hurl a second or third insult through the air. Then she tried to put her hand on the doorknob, but the other man smacked her hand away.

"You slobs, you're not supposed to hit a woman!" Aria exclaimed.

Both men started to chuckle. Aria pushed them aside and put her hand on the knob once again.

"Ay! I've got… I've… I've got an idea which can solve your problem," the man in the glasses suggested.

I was interested. "What is it?"

Aria turned to me and asked, "What the hell are you doing?"

The drunk man replied, "A game of riddles. If you win, you can enter the basement. But if we win, you have to… You have to strip naked and streak through the gala!"

Without a moment of hesitation, Aria whispered, "No, we're not doing that, Charles!"

Instead of listening to her, I thought to myself, *A game of riddles sounds like a random seventeenth century game. Why would those drunk men bother to pick riddles anyway? Why not Rock, Paper, Scissors or something like that?*

Eventually, since time was incredibly limited for us, I decided to take the offer instead of overthinking it.

"Alright," I agreed. "Who goes first?"

In response, Aria glared at me and whispered, "Charles!" with harshness in her voice.

The man in glasses pointed to himself. "I'll go first… The girl must answer the riddle."

He scratched his head and sat there like a rock. For a second, I though the man had fallen asleep until he suddenly jumped to wake himself back up.

"Well?" I asked. "We don't have all day."

The man looked up at Aria. "I've got it," he mumbled, giggling to himself.

She exhaled and said, "Then get on with it."

"Alright, alright," the man said, clearing his throat. "It shines during night and looks quite small, but touching it is possible from the ground with a jump."

Aria had to think for a moment.

"Well? Get on with it," the man mocked.

A few moments later, Aria exhaled and replied, "A firefly. That's the answer."

After a brief pause of silence, the man exclaimed, "Damn! That's right."

I leaned in and whispered, "How did you get that so quickly?"

She squinted. "Because the riddle was easy... It was barely even a riddle. It was basically a drunken description of a firefly."

Not wanting to admit it, I whispered to myself, "I thought that was kind of difficult..."

It was now my turn. In my mind, I would have decided that the drunk men would be able to tell a simple riddle or two, but they wouldn't be able to solve one.

"Alright, I have one."

The man with the boots replied, "I'm ready."

I said, "The monster of stone and eyes for hair now is headless for what man?"

After saying the riddle, I thought, *This riddle is difficult. There's no way he'll get it because it blends mythology with Greek history. He's just a drunk rebel; he has nothing in his head except for air. We've won... It's been assured.*

The man in the boots huddled against the door and rocked back and forth, acting just like Boney when he was alone in his room at night before we left for Salem Village.

"Ha!" the man in the boots screamed, startling me. "Perseus!"

What? That's right... How could he have guessed the answer so quickly? I thought. *He was even faster than Aria...*

Aria leaned in and whispered, "What was that?"

"What do you mean?"

"That wasn't a riddle."

I squinted my eyes at her. "What do you mean? That was a perfectly good riddle."

"That was a question you'd see on some sort of Greek mythology quiz about Medusa. That was not a riddle."

"Oh, whatever. I thought it was difficult."

Aria nodded her head and said, "Do you not know what a riddle is?"

The man in the boots straightened his back and chuckled, taunting me, for it was now his turn to give me a riddle.

"I have a good one," the man with the boots said. "I tick and tick making a sound, I break the barriers and the mountains with each minute passing by, what must I be?"

This seemed to piece together quite quickly.

Am I being a fool? It has to be a clock... I thought. *Or is this a trick?*

Suddenly, my senses flew into the memories which danced around in my head; the horror of the mines and all the turmoil the prison caused among the people in its possession. The answer wasn't a clock; the riddle was indeed a trick. The barriers and mountains were stone, and the ticks were the minutes that a miner would spend working his life away.

"A pickaxe!" I exclaimed. "The answer is a pickaxe!"

The man looked astonished.

"I... I'm impressed," he exclaimed. "I really am. That was a difficult riddle, even for me."

None of us had messed up just yet, although I was still concerned, not about Aria losing the game, but about the possibility that we could be discovered at any moment. Regardless of how the game was going, my paranoia wouldn't go away, especially after observing all the chaos that was now enveloping a once elegant fortress of wealth.

It was now Aria's turn to present her riddle to the man with the glasses. He said, "It's your turn, girl."

Aria replied, "Fine. I've got one."

"I'm ready!" the man with the glasses replied.

In a sarcastic voice, she said, "Alright, here it is... All shall bow by the waving symbol; it is the land's representation. What am I?"

I was confused; Aria's riddle was way too simple. The answer was a flag. So, as I had expected, the man with the glasses scratched his nose and said, "A flag, obviously."

Aria smirked and replied, "Incorrect."

Suddenly, the man leaped into the air and exclaimed, "What? How is that not the right answer?"

After a second of silence, Aria continued, "Your answer was incorrect. So, if you would, please get out of our way."

The two men stood still like they were frozen while Aria opened the door that led to the wine cellar. We took our first step down together, hearing all the echoes bouncing off the walls from behind us. As we were walking down the stairwell, I couldn't stop thinking about Aria's riddle.

"Aria, what was the answer?"

"A flag."

I was now even more confused. "But that was what the man said."

"Yup."

"Wait…" I mumbled. "So, you lied to them?"

"I did."

Aria's play had been intelligent, making a simple riddle and lying about the answer to get us out of there. It was a cheap move, but a brilliant one too.

After making our way down the steps, I realized that most of the bottles had been moved; they were all in the center of the room, waiting to be opened. We made our way to the pile, and I took a bottle from the top. Then I promptly removed the cap and turned it over, joyously watching the diamonds spill out across the floor.

"Wow… That's a lot of money," Aria marveled.

"It is," I replied. "Which is why we need to hurry up and get out of here."

After taking another bottle off the shelf, the door to the cellar slammed open and the voices of both drunk men bounced off the walls.

"You cheated!" one of the men yelled. "You cheated you lying cowards, and now you'll pay!"

One of the drunkards brought out his shotgun and fired it into the air, accidentally breaking one of the diamond bottles in the process. As they spilled all over the floor, the other man screamed, "You two are dead!"

27

The air inside the basement grew thicker and thicker by the second. Aria and I were sitting in a corner where darkness was the only thing protecting us from a pair of mad men who both had shotguns in their drunken grasp.

"See, this is what we get for cheating!" I complained.

"Oh please. Either way, we'd be in the same situation," Aria replied.

"Come on you two cowards, come out and fight us like real men!" the man with the boots exclaimed.

"What're we supposed to do?" I asked.

"Isn't it obvious?" Aria asked.

"No."

"We have to kill them."

"What?"

"If we don't, then we're going to be killed and I'd rather leave this place with my head intact!"

"No! We can't kill them."

Aria rolled her eyes and replied, "Fine, then we'll knock them out, you wuss."

Hesitantly, I replied, "Fine."

I didn't think the tables would turn so quickly. Aria and I weren't very far from being bandits at this point, now that we were stealing diamonds from a vault and attacking the guards who'd been alerted.

With our goal set into place, I snuck past a couple of the shelves, hoping I wouldn't run into anyone besides Aria. Then, as I turned a corner, I saw the man with the boots crouching, pointing his gun at anything that looked suspicious in the dark.

I have to distract them, I thought. *I can't let them find Aria.*

So, I grabbed a bottle of wine off the shelf and smashed it against the floor. Once the glass scattered across the darkness, the man leaped into the air and ran in my direction. In response, I ran farther away, losing sight of him in the process.

The man in the boots exclaimed, "I hear one of you, crawling and slamming your little toys against my floors. Come out!"

We were both silent; we were as silent as we could be. I couldn't see Aria which meant that she was either hiding or ready to strike.

Eventually, I slid behind another one of the shelves as the man with the boots turned in a random direction that was close to mine and fired. He missed, but almost hit me in the ear. As I looked over my shoulder, I saw a trail of broken glass and spilled some wine on the floor behind me.

"Did you get one of them?" the man with the glasses asked from across the room.

"How would I know?" the other man yelled.

"Just hit one of them already!"

"Alright, alright! Give me a second… goddamn."

I snuck past another bullet ridden shelf and saw the man with the boots facing the other way from it. Hoping to remain unnoticed, I tiptoed behind him and took another bottle from one of the shelves, holding it straight up in the air. As I approached him, the drunkard suddenly turned around and shoved the tip of his gun against the center of my forehead.

"There you are," the man in the boots mumbled, now smirking because of his victorious find.

He took a step forward and was now awfully close to me. His feet were about two feet away from mine which was also happened the full length of the shotgun barrel.

"Hey, I got him! I got one of those cheaters!" the man with the boots exclaimed.

"I'm still looking for the other one!" the man with the glasses yelled back. "Just keep him there, I wanna shoot the both of them together!"

One sudden thing happened after another. As I stood there, stiller than a pool in the midst of winter, Aria started to sneak up behind the man with the boots who was holding a shotgun up to my forehead. I grew silent and looked the man straight in the eyes as she would hopefully get rid of him.

"You're a pest," he said. "A really big pest… Just wait until that other pest is found. I can't wait to see your blood get all over the floors of this little room we've got down here."

Then the man with the boots looked at my hood.

"Say, who are you, anyway? I've… I've never seen you around here before."

"I don't know what you're talking about," I replied. "I'm just an ordinary guy."

"Are you now?"

"I am. I've been living here for quite a while now."

The man with the boots grew curious and touched the rim of my hood. Then he pulled it down and quickly realized who I was.

"Wait! You're that guy! The one everyone's looking to kill! You're him!"

"I don't see why," I replied. "I'm the one person in this city who's trying to get the hell out of here and leave it alone. Plus, it's not like I've done anything that's worth being killed over."

"You? Done nothing? You're the one who kicked out our true leader! You're a demon!"

Aria was now a step behind the man in the boots. She took a bottle of wine from the shelf to her left and steadily approached him. I heard the man talking to himself; he was astonished by my presence. With little time to spare, Aria took the bottle and smashed it over the man's thick skull. She dropped the rest of it and stared at the fallen body.

"You think he's still alive?" Aria asked.

I looked down at the man. His chest was slowly shifting up and down, so he was still breathing.

I replied, "It looks like it."

The man with the glasses continued to wander around the basement, but he was now alone. Aria stepped over the unconscious drunkard, and we tiptoed past another shelf. The man with the glasses seemed to be nowhere in sight. Aria and I both held two bottles full of diamonds and noticed the door wasn't very far from our reach.

She turned to me and whispered, "Let's lock him in. I doubt people will look down here if there's a gala going on upstairs."

I nodded and said, "That's a good idea."

The hallway toward the door seemed to be clear. I took the first step into plain sight and ran through the hallway with Aria. Seeing that the door was within our reach, we bolted up the remaining steps, causing a ruckus since the basement was always naturally quiet. As we reached the door, I heard the drunkard behind us load his shotgun.

"Hurry up, hurry up!" Aria exclaimed.

As per her request, we ran out of the basement and shut the door. Quickly after, we locked it and sprinted down the corridor to a neighboring room.

Suddenly, a crowd of noises flew right past us which made Aria and I turn our heads. More and more of the Greensburg rioters rushed to the main room since the gala was about to begin. Aria looked at the front door of the palace and next to it, she noticed a large mirror. As a result, she threw our hoods on, just before anyone in the new Greensburg community could recognize us.

After turning another corner in the palace's endless maze of hallways, I looked into the main room and saw all of the Greensburg civilians beginning to dance. To an extent, the gala seemed to be formally structured, but in a poor-formal kind of way. Everybody wore ragged clothes and old plastic jewelry. On top of that, nobody seemed to know how to dance. They were all jumping up and down or walking in circles; it was almost like they were trying to mimic a ritual to the underworld.

As the main room continued to fill up, Aria pulled me back and said, "When are we going to leave?"

I looked back at her and suddenly realized the difficulty of our situation.

"If we leave now, people will start to get suspicious. From what I've heard, everyone in the city will be here. So, if we leave now, someone could follow us out and ask where we're going."

"Hmm... Maybe. Then what are we supposed to do?"

"I think we should stay here for a little longer. We'll leave in the middle of the gala, so in about one hour. Maybe less. We can just sit in the corner and watch people dance until some people start leaving the palace. Then we can follow suit."

28

I stepped into the ballroom with Aria, even though I resented the idea of doing so. Nonetheless, the sight was nothing short of incredible. The only clothes people were wearing were all dirty and old, but the event on its own was much more thought out than I would have imagined. An orchestra performed on a stage which was off to the side of the room while everyone danced. Everyone's heads bobbed up and down to the music in an endless cycle of what looked like joy. Admittedly, this was the first time I saw the riot bonded by some form of peace.

Aria looked around nervously and I followed suit. We couldn't stand in the shadows since all the room was lit up to the level of the sun. So, we were forced to hide in plain sight again.

"How are we supposed to hide from everyone if we don't actually have anywhere to hide?" Aria asked.

I looked around at the people who were dancing. As we continued to shuffle past them, I replied, "What do you mean? We're hiding in plain sight. Just look around. Nobody's paying any attention to us. We'll be fine, just as long as we don't bring attention to ourselves."

Aria glanced at the center of the ballroom and replied, "Alright, but don't get into any trouble. I don't want to die just yet, especially because of you."

"I won't. Just calm down and have a drink or something. Better yet, keep watch of the entrance. If you see anyone else leave, we should be in the clear to follow them out."

Before long, more entertainment arrived. People in painted paper masks, along with some sort of mechanism made of wheels, entered the ballroom. Everything around us seemed to be a parade. But as the excitement of that parade reached its peak, the room suddenly grew quiet. A peculiar person who was surrounded by guards from the riot stood in the center of the parade line, waiting to be introduced. The crowd in the ballroom started to murmur and after a while stopped. During the mumbling, I heard the word "leader" spoken a couple of times, so I realized who that person was—the centerpiece of the entire parade.

Aria leaned over and whispered, "What's going on?"

"I don't have a good feeling about this."

The circle of guards expanded and the person from the parade line came into view; it was none other than Mrs. Jamison. Without taking another breath, I pulled my hood further down to where I could barely see.

Aria tugged on my sleeve and asked, "Who is that?"

Since I didn't want to explain the whole debt situation to her because of everything else that was going through my mind, I replied, "An enemy."

Mrs. Jamison stood up and smiled menacingly, extending her back to the point where she looked like a flagpole; for now, she didn't seem to notice me. I made my way to the far corner in the back of the crowd, now realizing the true severity of our situation.

"Hello everyone!" Mrs. Jamison started. "How are you all doing tonight?"

The crowd suddenly applauded her. Mrs. Jamison chuckled and thanked everyone, and then continued with her opening remarks.

"We've been working days and nights to find Charles Balkin, the traitor who killed Frederick Balkin, who is not only his own father, but a beloved leader and cherished friend."

The crowd continued to applaud her. In the middle of all the noise, I thought to myself, *So, that's what she's trying to do... She's getting rid of the Balkin name. That way, nobody else can take this city from her... And because of her, they all think I killed my father, and now they're trying to kill me. This is bad; I have to get out of here.*

"The economy of this city has fallen to its knees because of him."

What economy? I thought. *This isn't an actual city! What's she talking about?*

"So has our dignity as a nation!"

The crowd acted like animals; they were all mindlessly cheering, almost as if Mrs. Jamison was their God.

"But do not fear, my fellow liberators! We will soon find him and regain the dignity which Charles Balkin has stolen from us!"

Suddenly, I looked to my right and saw Aria vigorously stomping her foot against the floor like a bull; she was angry. Once Mrs. Jamison took her pause, everyone in the ballroom heard her. The rioters looked around until I touched Aria's hand, telling her to calm down. Once the noise coming from Aria's foot subsided, Mrs. Jamison cleared her throat and looked back at the crowd. She continued, "When this fool is captured—"

Suddenly, Mrs. Jamison was cut off again as Aria continued tapping her foot against the floor. She was clearly annoyed by Mrs. Jamison for making a mockery of my name, so this was her way of subconsciously showing it. In response, Mrs. Jamison's look grew serious, but after a few seconds of thought, it became clear that the distraction didn't seem to get to her. So, she continued with her speech and exclaimed, "This demon should be put to death! How could he do such a thing to Frederick—such a distinguished and thoughtful man? How could he kill our lea—"

In the moment, I decided to join Aria in her foot-stomping diversion. I saw her point; she wanted this distraction to spread like a disease among the rioters, which it did. Some of the other rioters in the crowd started to tap their feet as well, even though many of them were unsure of its purpose. Perhaps they assumed it was supposed to be some kind of new citywide tradition.

Mrs. Jamison continued, even though the noises from our feet were now clearly distracting her, "I believe that Charles left Salem Village about a day or two ago—"

The tapping echoed as the source continued.

"Oh my god! Would you quit that?" Mrs. Jamison yelled. "What are you all doing?"

In response, a burst of silence quickly overcame the ballroom.

"Uhm… Sorry," Mrs. Jamison mumbled. "Anyway, this demon will be taken by the neck and thrown into the dungeon the second we find him!"

I turned around and realized that Aria was still visibly angry. She was a very nice and quiet person for the entire time I'd known her, but something about Mrs. Jamison mocking my name, along with the entirety of this Greensburg riot, had changed her entirely. For some reason, this moment caused her to release a once hidden vein of anger that nobody had ever expected to see. Without a second to waste, Aria pushed toward the front of the crowd. Her hood fell and the rosy headband she wore revealed itself. Mrs. Jamison had never met Aria and I didn't think the two had known each other, so I was still safe.

Aria concluded her stampede at the front of the crowd and looked Mrs. Jamison straight in the eyes. As a dense cloud of tension rose between the two, she yelled, "First of all, who are you to say this man is a fool? Where's your proof? Who do you think you are to go around, spreading these horrible lies about a man who you sent to do your bidding? You're a coward, you know! If you wanted to get rid of Frederick so much, then why the hell didn't you just do it yourself?"

The crowd of rioters shifted their heads to Mrs. Jamison; we were all in shock. After taking just one glance at her face, everyone realized just how much her mood had flipped. This was especially clear after Mrs. Jamison exclaimed, "And just who do you think you are to come up here and interrupt me, you no-life peasant girl?"

Aria ignored her and yelled, "Charles didn't do this! You did! You're all lunatics for following her because she's the demon! She's the one who killed Frederick; I saw it all with my own eyes!"

Mrs. Jamison butted into Aria's outburst and said, "Whoever you are, I suggest you leave before I—"

Aria interrupted her again and continued, "This is all your fault! You people are the ones who should be thrown into the dungeon! You're the animals here!"

Once Aria finished screaming at most of the room, a pause of silence arose. Following that, a storm of boos and demands for Aria to be thrown in jail erupted from the heavens themselves. As I had expected, Mrs. Jamison followed the orders of the rioters and demanded, "Throw this psychopath into the dungeon!" after pointing at her makeshift guards.

Then, while Aria was whisked away to the abyss, Mrs. Jamison exclaimed, "Enjoy the gala, my great liberators. Let's enjoy the night while it's still young!"

An hour passed and people started leaving, even though the gala would go on for the rest of the night. As my chance to escape had finally presented itself, I whispered, "What the hell was she thinking? That idiot! She's like Victor. She said she would never be like him, and yet there she is, now in jail for a random outburst that she couldn't hold herself back from."

I was afraid for Aria. I didn't think she would even survive the city of Greensburg by itself, but now she had to survive a merciless dungeon within the city too. I had my doubts about her situation, thinking that she wouldn't live past the first week.

"What do I do?"

The music grew louder, so I couldn't hear my own whispers anymore.

Should I break into the dungeon? If I leave now, I'll still be able to make it back to Salem Village. I'll finally be free. But I can't just leave her here... Can I?

As I tried to deal with the dilemma at hand, Mrs. Jamison suddenly walked in front of the doorway. She turned around and gave me a clueless look.

"Hello there," she said.

I looked up at her and flinched. Then I made my voice deeper and replied, "Hello."

What? What the hell is she doing here in the back of the ballroom? Why is she talking to me? Did she figure out who I am?

The orchestra concluded their piece. The head violin turned the page in his music book and so did everyone else.

"You look shy," Mrs. Jamison continued. "I bet you're one of those people who are always in the back of the crowd during these types of celebrations."

Dammit! What should I do? I thought. *What kind of luck is this? Can this situation get any worse?*

I was forced to stay. This room was now a cage, one worse than Aria's.

"I guess you're right," I mumbled. I didn't know what else to say, mostly because of how panicked I was.

The next symphony started to play and all I wanted was for Mrs. Jamison to leave me alone. But just as luck would have it, Mrs. Jamison asked, "May I have this dance?"

No! No! No! God, why? Out of everyone in this world, why me?

I replied, "Of course, but I don't dance much."

"That fine! I can teach you."

This is bad. This is really, really bad.

I was led away from the doorway and straight into the middle of the ballroom by her right hand. Mrs. Jamison put her left hand on my shoulder and her other close to my hip. Then we embraced, joining the circle of dancers shifting left and right across the mud-showered room. As we continued waltzing with each other, she asked, "Do you like my dress?"

Mrs. Jamison was the only person in the entire city who had a dress that grabbed everyone's attention. It was the color of gold, and it had symbols from the prison written all over her waistline.

"Yes, of course," I replied. "It's beautiful."

She giggled and replied, "Thank you."

After dancing for a little while, she continued, "Why are you wearing a hood? Are you afraid to show me your face?"

I'm screwed... She wants to see my face. I have to change the subject. It doesn't matter what I change it to... I just need to change it to something! Come on... Think, Charles!

I ignored her previous remark and asked, "Do you ever think about the better parts of life?"

Mrs. Jamison was bewildered. "What do you mean by that?"

What did I just say? Was that even English?

I continued, "In other words... I doubt this 'Charles' guy is ever going to return to this city, so why do you want to capture him so badly anyw—"

Suddenly, Mrs. Jamison grabbed the rim of my hood and pulled it down.

"I knew it!" She exclaimed. "I knew it from the second I saw you standing around back here!"

The other rioters in the center of the ballroom turned around and gasped; by the sounds they were making, I realized just how angry they were.

"Take him to the dungeon with that other lunatic woman!" Mrs. Jamison demanded.

I exclaimed, "Wait... How did you—"

Mrs. Jamison interrupted me and said, "I'm not an idiot, Charles."

29

Two men who looked no different from the rest hustled me past a hallway into a dreary cellar, one that was consumed by an unsettling white noise. As the guards dragged me across the floor, I saw an opened cage in front of me with Aria sitting inside. They threw me inside, and then proceeded to lock it.

The cell seemed to be old and hollow. I could hear pipes leaking in the distance and echoes slowly bouncing off the walls from the quiet muttering of the other captives. While I left Boney, Griff, and Miss Annabelle behind at Salem Village, Aria sat in one corner of the cell while I was in the other.

"They found you?" Aria mumbled.

"Obviously."

"How?"

"I don't know... For some reason, Mrs. Jamison wanted to dance with me and a few seconds later, she—"

"Do you mean the cult leader?"

"Yeah, her."

"Have you ever met her before?"

"Back when I was in prison."

"Wait, what? She was also a prisoner?"

I replied, "No... It's a long story," and then told her how I met Mrs. Jamison.

Several hours had passed. A strange man walked past our cell, holding some sort of rusted can. Once he made his way back to the dungeon entrance, he stumbled upon us. As I looked up at him, I realized just how much his yellow hat added brightness to the room.

He placed the can onto the ground and reached for a tiny spoon. After the man placed it onto the ground, he took two smaller cans and placed them both on the floor. Since the silence between us was awkward, I decided to start some conversation.

"I like your hat," I said.

The old man smiled, revealing his one lone tooth. "Thank you."

I smiled back at him. Then, as he poured us our food, he continued, "You two seem surprisingly nice. Every time I'm forced to feed the prisoners down here, I usually get yelled at."

"I'm not surprised. I mean… What else would you expect?"

"You're right," he said. "Nonetheless, I don't judge the people down here. I doubt they're sinister. They're just stressed from being locked up."

"Sure. That's a good way to look at it."

As the old man fiddled with the spoons, he continued, "You know, some of the people down here are fans of you, including myself."

"You know me?"

"How could I not? You've been the talk around this city ever since the day you kicked Marcus out of the palace and sent Frederick off to trial. You know, the one by Salem Village?"

"Yeah, I was there. He looked like he had gone insane by the end of the trial; you should've seen it. He tried to attack the judge with a knife. Good thing he's in prison now, rotting away behind bars just like me. I'm surprised she's telling everyone that I killed him, though. I don't think I'd ever have the guts to do that."

The old man seemed to be shocked.

"Didn't you hear?" the old man asked. "That Jays guy was proven to be insane. He was sent to an asylum a few days after the end of the trial."

"Really?"

"Yeah. One of the town's people there proved that Jays was the one who burned down that psychic's place. Turns out some kid got the whole thing on video. Jays lit the psychic's place on fire after she rejected him."

So, it looks like Mrs. Jamison's plan failed.

"But I thought Frederick burned it down…"

The old man continued, "I'm pretty sure he admitted to framing Frederick for burning down the shop after they brought him to the asylum."

"That's terrible."

"It's not all one-sided, though." The old man continued, "Frederick's still going to prison for two years for trying to attack the judge with a knife."

The old man took the spoon and started to ladle some soup into the two smaller cans. The swill was dirty, and the potatoes seemed to be rotten. Only half of each can was filled.

"Anyway, I gotta go. My time's up for today," the old man exclaimed.

"Going to the gala?" I asked.

"God, no. I hate dancing."

"Why's that?"

He didn't reply.

Then the old man scattered but left the rest of the soup on the ground. Before passing through the front door, he looked back at me and smiled.

The second day in the cell proved to be harder than the first. I started to draw random pictures on the wall with a small pebble I found near the bars because there was nothing else to do. The can which the old man left behind was empty and useless by now.

Soon, Aria woke up with a gloomy look; she looked like a phantom who was slowly fading away in the darkness. The air grew thick like the air of a graveyard; we were both falling out of reality, not knowing what to do with ourselves.

In a tired voice, I mumbled, "Wow, you look grim."

"Of course, I am."

Aria looked like she was thinking about something, so I asked her, "What are you thinking about?"

"My mother. She's back home in the village."

"Is she alright?"

"Yes."

"So why are you thinking about her?"

"I don't know."

"Are you alright?"

"I'm fine... I just look like this because I had a bad dream."

"Do you want to talk about it?"

Aria looked at the ground and hugged her own knees. "I saw a few images of my mother. The rioters forced her to dig her own grave past the Greensburg cemetery while the rest of my family had to watch."

Dear god, what kind of dream is that?

"That really is grim."

"I swear… I'm going insane. That's exactly what this cell's doing to me."

The effects of Greensburg had finally taken effect on her. Aria was the first victim of the Greensburg phantom's evil transcendence. Her hair started to puff, and she would grow skinnier by the day. Soon enough, Aria's growing madness got the best of me too.

By now, I would have thought that Boney, Griff, or anyone else in Salem Village would be worried for me. I told them that I would return in two days with Aria safe at home, but because we were captured, I thought they might have forgotten about us.

A full week passed without serenity or rest. I sat in the corner with Aria every day, doing nothing at all. My eyes were slowly turning red while hair started covering the skin under my nose. The only part of the day where insanity didn't overtake the cell was the single conversation I would have with the old man who delivered supper.

It was close to dinnertime. I sat at the edge of the cell where I was able to touch the floor of the hallway. I waited. Nobody was there. I stroked my hand against the floor, and I was able to hear my hand make contact with the concrete. I assumed that the old man wasn't on time for his shift.

Another hour had passed. Supper time was now fading into the darkness of the abyss.

"Hello?" I yelled. "Is anyone there?"

The message repeated several times and nobody responded to me. I looked at the other cells and each of them looked empty.

"Charles, do you not see what's happening here?" Aria asked.

"What do you mean?" I replied, clenching my fists.

I was talking calmly, trying to hold back the anger which wanted to erupt.

"The old man isn't coming back—"

I stopped Aria as somebody was walking in the distance.

"He's here!" I exclaimed.

The person in the distance arrived, except he wasn't the old man. He was a young boy who looked gloomy and confused. His shoes were dull like the yard where Aria had envisioned her mother digging her own grave.

The boy walked up to our cell and performed the same feeding ritual the old man had performed for us.

"Where's the old man?" I asked.

The boy ignored me. He took two rusty cans and threw them onto the floor. The meal for today seemed to be different; rather than soup, he served us two soggy pieces of meat.

"What kind of meat is that? Beef? Lamb? Or something else, like a—"

I was cut off when the boy slid our food to us through the bars. The contents spilled and turned darker from all the dirt and paint which was slowly crumbling off the walls. Even though I was reluctant, I grabbed a piece and took a bite. The food was raw.

"What is that?" I repeated. "This is disgusting."

The boy replied, "The old man."

I looked down at the spilled meat, now confused.

"I don't understand. What about the old man?"

The boy was about to leave when he replied, "You're eating him."

I swallowed the piece of meat and realized my sin. Aria stopped and started to cry after realizing what we had put into our hands. Our souls were now tainted; our sanity was quickly fading away.

30

We ate all the old man's meat because Mrs. Jamison had stopped sending people over to feed us, although the same little boy would come by every now and then to deliver the remnants of someone's bath water. By now, I was certain that our time to die was steadily approaching.

As always, Aria continued to sit in her corner while the hallways remained dark. She eventually fell asleep while I remained awake. All I could do that night was look at the mold which was slowly growing from the side of the cell.

After two weeks of solitude and virtually no food, I felt like an animal. All I ate were old leftovers and bugs which would occasionally run around the cell walls. Sometimes, when I could only find one, I had to rip it apart and give the other half to Aria. The taste was terrible. We would throw up and re-eat what we had lost at times because we couldn't find anything else to live off.

When Aria woke up, I was relieved because it was difficult to tell whether she was sleeping or dead.

"You look pale," I pointed out.

She couldn't lift her head.

"I'm going to die soon. I know it," She replied.

"No. You'll be fine—"

"Sure… When I'm finally down in purgatory."

"Why would you say such a thing?"

Then, from out of nowhere, she mumbled, "Listen, Charles… I've been thinking about this for the past few days now and… And I want you to kill me."

Aria slowly reached into her back pocket. She was barely alive; I was pretty sure that she could only move the top half of her right arm. By now, she was only a mere skeleton.

After holding still for a while, she took a sharp piece of glass from the floor after having dropped it earlier. Aria held it up, knowing I would see it in the clearest light of the cell.

"Aria, stop acting like a lunatic. We'll get through this."

"Please… I'm begging you. I'm more dehydrated than a dead flower. I'm crippling from the pain. It hurts, and I don't want to go through this anymore."

Aria dropped the piece of glass onto the floor again.

"No, Aria—"

"Do it."

"You're being unreasonable."

As the dungeon grew completely silent, Aria replied, "Charles… If you don't kill me, then I'll do it myself."

The piece of broken glass came from the bottle of wine she had used to knock out the drunk man.

"Please…" she continued with a voice drier than the Sahara in the summer. "You can use me for food. You'll live longer and I'll be happy in the arms of God… That is, if he lets me sleep in peace. So, there's a chance… Maybe we'll all win."

Aria looked at the glass shard that was now in my hands. She closed her eyes while mine were staring into the reflection of an animal.

In an annoyed voice, I replied, "No! Where is this all coming from, anyway?"

"Stop being a coward," she replied, ignoring my last question. At this point, I could barely hear her because of how dry and empty her voice was.

"Just calm down and sit back. We'll get our chance to escape."

Then, as if Poseidon himself had come down from out of nowhere to strike my eyes with his golden scepter, I started sobbing. At first, I had no idea why, but after looking into Aria's half-opened eyes and her dried up body, I realized what these tears had truly meant to me.

"Why are you crying?" She said.

I stayed silent.

After pausing, she brushed up against my shoulder and whispered, "Stop being afraid. You know what I want. So, make me happy and do it."

In response, I whispered, "You don't know what'll make you happy because you're losing your head."

With what strength she had left, Aria groomed her right hand up against my thigh and muttered, "Yes, I do."

"What about your mother, Aria? She'll miss you. Your family will miss you."

Aria coughed and laughed at the same time. "I lied about my mother… She died when I was six. My father joined her two years after. I'm alone, so I wanted to make myself seem happy. I was always alone, even when I met you and everyone else. I've never really—"

"You know, you're really starting to piss me off."

After losing her train of thought, she wiped the last tear off my face and continued, "Do it then. Take out your anger on me and let me die."

Suddenly, she started to cry as well. A storm of muddy water cascaded down her cheeks, only to hit my knees in the process. "Let me join my mother and father in heaven. I can't stand this anymore. Let me die. You don't know how long I've wanted to—"

And just like that, I took a black shard from the abyss and slit her throat in one fell swoop. She dropped faster than her tears, and for the rest of the night, I sat there, joining her corpse in the act of nothingness.

When the morning came, my stomach rumbled. As my head started to hurt, I slouched my back and leaned against the wall. With the little amount of energy I had left in my legs, I stood and took a step closer to her corpse. With the piece of blood covered glass that I loosely grasped in my right hand, I started to cut her open like a butcher slicing open a pig's belly. Then I closed my eyes and grabbed something; I wasn't sure what part of her body I was holding, but I knew it was red. Upon taking my first bite, I felt like a true animal— there was no going back for me.

Later that week, after staring at her skull for what felt like a century, I picked it up and observed it. As my voice grew dull, I whispered, "I'm sorry…" and gently placed it on the ground. At that very moment, I turned around and saw one of the bones from her arm suddenly fall onto the floor. After bending down and caressing it with my dry fingertips, I realized just how lucky I was to have accepted Aria's sacrifice.

Even though I had little to no strength left in my legs, I took the bone and limped across the cell. I reached for the lock and stuck Aria's remnants inside. After fiddling with it for some time, I heard a noise appear from the darkness. *Click.*

The cell door flew open. I fell to my knees and crawled into the hallway.

31

I walked along the center of the hallway. Each step I took led me closer to the gates that would finally allow me to leave this spinning image of Hell. Once I reached the end of the hallway, I found the door to the dungeon and tried to open it, only to realize that it was locked.

Suddenly, I heard a voice coming towards me from the other side. The doorknob started to shake. Without much time to spare, I limped to a corner of the room and hid, now carefully watching the entrance.

Once the door opened, two large men entered; it was the two intoxicated men who Aria had fooled in the riddle game.

The man with the boots said, "You think those cheaters are still alive?"

The man with the glasses chuckled and replied, "I doubt it."

Then they both laughed and walked down the hallway, holding their shotguns in one hand and a wine bottle in the other. I started to tiptoe behind them to find my way out. But when the two men blended into the darkness, I started running.

After I made my way out of the dungeon, I grabbed the edge of the door and slammed it shut.

As I walked through the empty hallways of the palace, I was curious to see what happened during my imprisonment. So, after wandering around for a while, I stepped out onto the balcony which faced the rest of Greensburg. The light blinded my eyes just as much as the time when I escaped the prison with Boney and everyone else. Upon first glance, Greensburg looked different from how it was one month ago. The palace was clean, and the homes looked peaceful again. The sun overlooked the town with a burst of resounding light while a bunch of citizens ran from one building to another.

As I turned away from the facade of Greensburg, I could suddenly hear a series of footsteps heading towards the balcony. After turning around, I found Mrs. Jamison standing under the balcony entrance without a single guard by her side.

"Hello, Charles," she said.

She sounded casual. Not a hint of fear or anxiousness was in her voice.

"'Hello, Charles,' is all you have to say after throwing me into that dungeon? What's wrong with you?" I exclaimed.

"Charles…"

"No! Don't say my name! You don't deserve to say my name!"

"Calm down."

"You made me eat my friend! You made me—"

"Calm down!"

Both of us grew silent.

I took a step closer to Mrs. Jamison and looked her in the eye, not knowing what she wanted from me because I had nothing left to offer her. Back in the prison, she had taken every bit of wealth I owned, and now she did the same in Greensburg. She took everything from me, including Aria.

"You know, you're quite good at escaping prisons," she marveled. "I'm impressed."

"Shut up," I replied.

In response, Mrs. Jamison turned around and walked inside. I wasn't sure if I should have followed her or not, but I did.

"What are you doing?" I continued. "Where are you going?"

She opened a drawer and pulled out a small, olive-colored envelope which had a giant red stamp in the center; the very same symbol I couldn't seem to run away from. Mrs. Jamison handed me the envelope and closed the drawer. She looked at me and smiled.

"What's this?"

"Open it and see. You are allowed to indulge every once in a while, you know."

I looked down at the envelope and slid the tip of my nail against the seal to open it. Then I unfolded the contents, noticing today's date written at the top, and started to read.

Dear Charles,

When you were younger, I created the prison as a part of the Greensburg utopian plan. This idea was formulated to represent the good in people. I wanted to make a perfect city where the civilians wouldn't have any worries or stress consuming their lives—one where we could bathe in diamonds and wine and all the other things that we could blissfully have both on earth and the heavens.

Greensburg seemed like a good idea at the time. It really did. But after seeing all the madness that you've created, this utopian experiment has officially turned into a failure. Nonetheless, that doesn't mean I won't continue this little experiment of mine. If it is truly necessary, I'll make a 'Greensburg Two'; perhaps even a 'Greensburg Three'. I'll make a hundred Greensburg cities if I have to, all for the sake of my utopian dream.

And if you ever have the urge to stop me in my path ever again, I'll send you back to that prison. If anything, I'll build a new prison just for you and send you there so you can live alone for the rest of your life. So, I advise you to take my words heavily: run back down into the crevices of our planet, deeper than the ocean trenches and the mantle itself, and leave my work and my life out of your hands, because if our eyes lock ever again, even just for a second, I'll make sure to flip your skin inside-out.

Anyway, enjoy what's left of your sanity.

Sincerely,

Frederick Simpson Balkin.

I looked up at Mrs. Jamison and asked, "What is this?"

"Your father wrote this for you a few years ago," she replied. "He was confident that you would escape the prison one day, so he left this here for you as a form of advice. And, of course, you failed to follow it…"

32

I folded the letter to the point where I couldn't the ink bleed through it anymore. Then I handed it, along with the envelope, back to Mrs. Jamison.

"Well Charles, it looks like it's time for you to return to the prison. You should be grateful that your father is such a forgiving man; usually in situations like these, you'd already be dead."

I responded with nothing but silence.

"Come on, say something. I can't wait here all day for you to talk to me. I'm a busy woman, after all."

Mrs. Jamison walked through a door which led into an empty corridor. I followed her, ignoring almost every word she'd said along the way. As I took my first step past the door frame, all the memories from the prison returned. I thought about all the people down there who were still searching for me after I escaped them with Victor. Then I remembered the mines and how they'd taken all my wealth; that had been my motivation for leaving the caves in the first place.

Eventually, Mrs. Jamison led me into the front yard of the palace where she faced me to say a final goodbye. A carriage was on the other side of the gate, waiting for me to enter. I couldn't see who the driver was, but that didn't seem to matter because Mrs. Jamison made me focus on her instead of the carriage.

"You're one special man, you know that? After all that's happened to you, I'm surprised that you're still alive."

I regretted coming back to Greensburg. The only reason I had come back was for those damned diamonds... But now everything was falling apart. I was officially trapped in the worst-case scenario of my reality.

In response to Mrs. Jamison's remark, I mumbled, "Why do I have to go back to those caves? Why can't you just leave me alone? I don't plan on ever coming back here, anyway."

To a certain extent, I felt like we were being too nice to each other given our past. Realistically, I could tell that she resented me just by the faint glare in her eyes.

"Frederick is the one who decides where you go and what you do. And as per his orders, I have to send you back to the prison."

"But… Wait, didn't you try to get rid of him? I don't understand… Why are you following his orders when you tried to get rid of him—"

"I hope you enjoy the ride back to the station. The view on the way is quite nice."

And then the lightbulb in my head flickered on. I ignored her last remark and said, "Let me guess… My father didn't actually write the letter you just gave me."

I looked back and saw the man in the carriage climb off his seat; it was Mr. Gliss. He waved at me.

Mrs. Jamison smirked at me and continued, "Goodbye, Charles. I trust that you won't try to escape, because if you do… Well, you read my letter. You know what will happen to you."

I glared at her as a couple of guards ran out from the front doors of the palace and escorted me past the gate. They set me onto the carriage where I was now in the shadows of Mr. Gliss.

The carriage started to move forward as Mrs. Jamison waved me off.

"Goodbye!" Mrs. Jamison exclaimed.

"Go to hell you heartless, half-brained, lying shrew!" I screamed.

After saying my final goodbye, I was on my way to the station. The carriage was set along a pathway which was different from the earlier one. I didn't seem to recall these parts of Greensburg. The fields were still beautiful, though; they were filled with daisies and trees while the sun showered them grass in its golden energy.

Mr. Gliss looked back at me, knowing that the pathway to the train was straight ahead. He said, "It's nice to see you again, Charles."

"It's nice to see you too."

This was the final chance I had before the caves trapped me in solitude again. I didn't want to end up like Boney, a sick and frail old man who spent his retirement in the caves, so I had to move quickly, regardless of how weak my body was from sitting around in Mrs. Jamison's cell for a full month.

I asked, "How long until we get to Salem Village?"

Mr. Gliss squinted at me; he was bewildered. "Pardon?"

I laughed a little. "This was your plan all along, right? You came back from Salem Village just to save me, and now you're taking me back."

"Uhm… Charles, I can't do that."

By the tone of his voice, I knew Mr. Gliss wasn't joking around with me.

"What do you mean? I thought we were friends."

"If I take you back there, they'll hunt me down and kill me."

"That's no problem. We can run away to a different part of the state; maybe even a different state. They'll never catch us."

He looked away.

"Mrs. Jamison will find you, anyway. Even if you run off to a different state, they'll find you and force you back into that prison. And then they'll kill me for helping you run away."

"Mr. Gliss... There's no need for betrayal here. Let's not start making up theories—"

"Sorry, Charles. I really am. I'm just not ready to die yet, especially for a client."

As my desperation grew exponentially, I reached into my jacket pocket and pulled out a handful of diamonds; they glimmered beautifully in the sunlight, which made them even more treacherous.

"Mr. Gliss?"

"Yes?"

He turned around and saw the diamonds stacked high in my hand.

"What is it?" He continued.

"Take it. You'll be richer than anyone in your family; you'll be able to retire from this carriage business too... Or at the very least, you'll be able to buy yourself a real car."

He turned around.

"I don't take bribes."

Fine, I thought. *If you don't want to help me, then we're enemies.*

I didn't continue the conversation. Instead, I bent down and hid under Mr. Gliss' seat. Then, for the next minute or so, I remained silent, pretending as if I'd somehow jumped out of the carriage. Once my silence became somewhat unsettling to the driver, Mr. Gliss asked, "Charles?"

He turned around and I was sure he didn't see me because the carriage had suddenly stopped.

"Charles?" He exclaimed. "I don't want to play games right now!"

Gliss' feet stomped onto the dirt path. I heard loud footsteps slowly approaching me on the right side of the road. Once Mr. Gliss reached the edge of the carriage, I jumped out and pushed him inside.

"Charles, what are you doing?" He continued.

"I'm not coming back! I'm not going back to that damned prison! Never!"

"Charles, wait!"

I took out the bloodied shard of glass that I used to butcher Aria and held it high in the air.

"And don't follow me. If you do… I'll slit your throat! I'll do it, Mr. Gliss!" I exclaimed while running across the path.

"Get back here, Charles! Get back here!"

His voice was incredibly stern; he was frightened, yet angry at the same time.

"Go to hell, Mr. Gliss! I thought I could trust you, but I guess you're no better than the rest of those Greensburg animals!"

I ran to the point where the carriage was far out of my sight. I didn't know if Salem Village was an option anymore because Mrs. Jamison would most likely hire a search squad to go there and look for me. So, I didn't have any other choice but to run away; I had to run away from Massachusetts and perhaps the rest of the north.

Later that night, I found myself walking through a forest in the dark. Salem Village seemed to be quite far away now; at least, I hoped so. I decided that going anywhere nearby would be a mistake, so the forest would be my new home for the time being. There would be no cages or cells; no caves; nothing except the freedom of soaring boards and leaves hanging off the trees. Autumn had finally arrived, so the leaves were falling, and the air was calm. A carpet of yellow and orange colors covered the ground as the crescent-shaped moon started to reveal itself across the ground.

I arrived at a large stone bordering a river, so I cupped my hands together and drank from the stream. For once, I didn't taste bacteria in the water; there wasn't one noticeable problem with my surroundings, nothing at all. I took a seat on the rock and observed the water flowing past my bare feet. I didn't want to follow the river for fear it could lead me back into Greensburg. Soon, I fell asleep.

Morning struck once again, and I was alone. I enjoyed the quiet air filtering through the forest and the birds chirping away at each other from above the pines. I stood and looked around; everything seemed pleasant.

Suddenly, I heard a voice calling my name from the distance. It startled me, so I instinctively hid behind the stone that I'd slept on throughout the night. As I poked my head out into the air, I saw Mr. Gliss; he was now at the riverside, walking in circles like a lost deer.

He yelled, "Charles? Charles?" and continued to walk through the forest. "Please, Charles! Just come out and listen to me for a minute!"

I stood and snuck behind his path, creeping behind each tree he passed along the way.

Is Mr. Gliss really my enemy now? Does he deserve to be my enemy? He seemed like such an innocent man. Surely, he wasn't deserving to be threatened by death. But I also had to think for myself.

Should I warn him again to leave me alone?

Finally, I jumped out behind him and mumbled, "Why are you still following me?"

I could see the startled look on his ghostly face as he turned around. When our eyes met, he reluctantly took a step forward and begged, "Charles… They're going to kill me. Please… Just come with me."

"No."

"Please, Charles… I'll do anything—"

"I said no."

Mr. Gliss hesitated. He couldn't reply because he was afraid of his fate.

"I'm begging you…"

He couldn't finish his sentence, so I finished it for him. "This is our final goodbye, Mr. Gliss. As much as I hate to say this, I hope I never have to see you again."

"Please…" Mr. Gliss wept.

I couldn't hear the rest of his sentence because I was already too far away. I didn't look back, but I knew Mr. Gliss was far behind. I heard his tired breaths; they were slowly fading away.

33

The riverbank ended by the edge of the forest. The moon in the twilight fog was pale and Mr. Gliss was nowhere to be seen. The river flowed into a lake which was glimmering in the moonlight. I sat down along the edge of the water where I grasped a rock and felt it; it was smooth and calming by the likes of the lake. I took the stone and skipped it over the top of the water, making it bounce once or twice before eventually plummeting into the darkness.

I thought to myself, *where do I go now? What should I do? Should I try to find Boney and Miss Annabelle and Griff? Are they even looking for me?*

I grabbed another stone and skipped it against the water. After it skipped across the water a few times, I heard a *clink*.

What could that possibly be? I thought. "Hello, is anyone there?"

I took another stone and skipped it across the water in the same direction and I heard the *clink* noise once again. The sound came from glass, I was sure of that.

I continued looking around until I saw a faint white light in the distance. My curiosity had gotten the best of me, so I stood and circled the water. After running by the lakeside, I stumbled upon a small glass bottle which was sitting firmly on the grass. It was clean, and a rolled-up piece of paper was inside. As my curiosity piqued, I grasped the bottle and vigorously pulled on the cork. But it was no use; the bottle wouldn't open because I was too weak. So, I thought and thought until the simplest idea of all came to mind. I smashed the bottle against a nearby tree and watched the glass shatter in front of my very eyes. Then I unfurled the note and read:

To my greatest love, Rose.

Oh, how deserving you are of life and happiness, my dear. Each of your eyes sparkle brighter than a ruby, day and night. Your hair is a sweet definition of honey. Your beauty truly overwhelms me.

Please, my dear, will you allow me to visit you by the lakeside? We've been writing to each other for six years now and I deserve to witness you in person.

Love,

Sylvester Franklin

I took a glance at the back of the page where a portrait of a man was drawn. He had a slight beard and pale eyes, and, to my surprise, looked very familiar when I raised the drawing up to the moonlight for a clearer view. Then it came to me; the portrait was none other than Boney in his younger form, whose real name seemed to be Sylvester Franklin.

"What's this doing in a lake?" I thought to myself. "Is that really Boney? Or is that someone who looks like him?"

I folded the paper and threw it into my jacket which now felt somewhat like a vault of sorts, holding diamonds and a note revealing a piece of Boney's past.

"It has to be him," I continued, "The man looks just like him, only younger."

This coincidence seemed too good to be true. If I would've run the slightest point off course from the lake, I would've never found the bottle. Eventually, this logic led me to the question: was this some kind of trap? Was Mrs. Jamison using Boney to reel me back into her grasp like a trout stuck to a fishing line? As my paranoia grew, I turned around and started to run. The moonlight faded as I ran deeper into the forest that night.

After a night of hiding in the trees, I decided that I wanted to visit my friends again, no matter the risks I would have to face. I don't exactly know what drove this craving of mine; perhaps I was just lonely, or perhaps I was enticed by the possibility that I would be able to revive Boney's past if I could show him the love letter I'd just found.

Regardless of the reason, I was on my way back to Salem Village. If Boney was still alive, I could finally remind him of his real name, given that the bottle wasn't some kind of petty trap. When I took the love letter and unfolded it again, I studied it along the way. As the sun started to rise, the daylight quickly became a helpful magnifying glass. I stopped by the rock where I had sat earlier, and Mr. Gliss was nowhere to be seen. The boulder felt no different than before and the water trickling down from the leaves constantly hit the top of my head. The letter was safe from the water, but it wasn't safe from me. I studied each corner of the image and each letter more carefully than a biologist looking under a microscope. I observed the city address at the top of the page which was unfamiliar to me: Albany, New York.

Suddenly, an idea struck me. Instead of finding Boney in Salem Village, why not find this Rose woman in Albany? If she was indeed real, then I would be assured that this bottle was not one of Mrs. Jamison's traps. So, I stood and reached into my jacket. I pulled out a small gray compass, pointing in the direction of Albany. I knew where Albany was because Mr. Gliss had once shown me a map of Massachusetts and pointed out the direction from Greensburg to New York. This was back when I still controlled the palace.

Without another moment to waste, I started to run past the red oaks. The grass was still the same color as it was the night before and there was barely a single leaf left on the trees.

It was now the middle of the day because the sun stood directly over my head. I grabbed a handful of water from a nearby puddle and drank. After quenching my thirst, I looked up and saw a light in the distance; it was bright enough to be visible from afar during the daytime.

I walked out of the forest and into a clear grass field, slowly sneaking my way toward the light. As I continued to hide behind a tree near the edge of a forest, a train entered the area on a set of tracks and a depot. This was a different train from the one in Greensburg; the windows looked clean and the people outside were excited to board. The conductor stepped outside and greeted the line of passengers who were joyfully waiting. The children were all gathered up and playing with the leaves; they were jumping and screaming, doing the things a child would typically adore in the Fall.

The conductor exclaimed, "We'll be boarding for Albany in five minutes! Please gather your children and make sure you have your tickets."

Albany? I thought. *What kind of coincidence is that?*

"All aboard!" The conductor continued.

Whatever, I have to get on that train! This is my chance!

I put my hood up. People were forming a line, so I slipped into the crowd. However, as I was standing in line, I came to the realization that I didn't have a ticket. I may have had time to buy one if I didn't spent so much time hiding behind the trees.

Since I didn't have a ticket, I'd have to buy one off somebody else. In a moment of growing desperation, I looked at the woman in front of me. She was tall and pale and wore a red headband. Her children stood at her side, all of whom were holding hands. There was a stack of blue tickets in her back pocket, so I tapped her shoulder and asked, "Sorry, but is there any chance you've got another ticket you'd be willing to sell to me?"

The woman turned around as her hair flew back. "No, sorry."

I looked at her in disappointment and replied, "Alright. Thank you."

However, as I turned away, the woman grasped my shoulder and continued, "I don't have any spare tickets, but I'm sure I can sneak one of my kids in."

Suddenly, my eyes widened. "Wow, thank you, I appre—"

"Hold on a second," She continued. "I'll only give you one of my tickets if you do me a small favor."

Of course, I was curious, so I responded by saying, "Sure, what is it? I'll pay you back for the ticket if you want."

"No, I don't need you to do that," she said. The woman then pointed to a man in the crowd and continued, "Do you see my husband over there?"

I turned around and saw a tall man leaning against a log. He didn't look at his wife for the past couple of minutes, even though a flock of strangers were surrounding her and their children. The man was wearing black suspenders and a brown leather fedora. He was holding a suitcase made of brown leather and wore a pair of black shoes.

"The guy with the hat?" I asked.

"Yes, him."

"Alright. And what do you want me to do?"

"Do you see that hat he's wearing?"

"Yes," I replied.

"I want you to get rid of it. Then I'll give you one of my tickets."

"You want me to destroy your husband's hat? Why?"

"Oh, don't even get me started... He loves that damned thing more than me. I've been with that loathsome man for twelve years now and all he ever talks about is that stupid hat!"

"Well, alright... I doubt it'll be that difficult."

"Thank you, honey."

The conductor was near the front of the train going about his business. I walked over and stood next to the woman's husband as a sudden burst of nervousness traveled through my veins. He wore a nametag: Jared. Jared's wife told me that he was a salesman, so he always had to wear a name tag for his clients.

I looked back and forth between his fedora and the ground, tapping my foot against the grass as I thought about my plan. But of course, I didn't have one, so I eventually decided to improvise.

As the line to enter the train grew shorter, I looked up at Jared and said, "Wow, I just noticed your fedora and I really like it."

He turned his head and looked down at me.

"Oh, thank you. It's an original from the nineteenth century. I think it was made in 1896."

I kept hesitating. Whenever he looked down at me, the air grew colder.

Finally, I said, "How about I buy it from you? I'm a collector."

"Are you? I do like fellow collectors, but I can't sell this one. It's too rare," he replied. "And I just happen to like it too much."

I reached into my jacket and took out a handful of diamonds.

"How about this?"

"Sorry. I can't help you."

I turned my head and the conductor yelled, "All aboard!" one last time.

The line started to move, and Jared said, "I'll see you on the train."

I was running out of ideas and time, so I panicked and suddenly grabbed the hat off his head. However, as I started to run, Jared knocked me to the ground and laughed.

"Bet my wife bribed you. It's happened before."

34

I stood as Jared grabbed my shoulder and fixed up my hair, all while the line started to move. It was lengthy, stretching from the entrance of the train to the back of the station by the woods.

"Listen," Jared said. "I'll help get you onto this train, unlike my scheming wife."

"Thank you… That means you have a ticket to spare, right?" I replied.

"God no, if I had the money to be buying all of these tickets, I'd be taking first-class down to Florida."

"So, then how are you going to get me on the train?"

"I'll tell one of my children to hide behind my leg when we enter the train. I'll make sure the conductor doesn't see him."

I shook Jared's hand and exclaimed, "Thank you so much!"

He gave me his youngest son's ticket and I clamped it in my grip.

"Now, since I gave you that ticket, you owe me something," he declared.

What? I thought, now annoyed.

Reluctantly, I replied, "Alright."

"Take a look at my wife."

I exhaled and said, "I'm looking at her," following Jared's finger with my eyes as he pointed forward.

He said, "Do you see that red headband she's wearing?"

"Of course, I do."

"I want you to get rid of it."

You've got to be kidding me.

"Her headband?"

"Yes," he said. "That will be my revenge for her for trying to take away my fedora."

I walked up to Jared's wife who was waiting to enter the train. She seemed to forget about me until I'd grabbed her shoulder.

"Did you that fedora I asked for?" the woman asked, showing some excitement.

"No, but I was able to get a ticket of my own. Sorry about that."

"That's quite alright. If you want, you're welcome to join us in our booth. I'd love the extra company."

"Sure, thanks."

The conductor smiled as I passed him, entering the wagon which had lightly stained windows from the inside and gloomy yellow carpets covering the aisles. I took another step and followed the couple I'd met in line. When we made our way to the end of the aisle, I slid into the booth after their children, along with Jared and his wife.

"So, what's your name?" I asked.

"Oh, I'm Sabrina. It's nice to meet you."

What a coincidence, I thought. *Isn't that the psychic's name from Salem Village?*

"Sabrina? The name sounds familiar," I said. "Have we met somewhere before?"

Sabrina sat up tall and replied, "Hmm… I don't think so."

After a few seconds of silence, she continued, "Maybe we've met at my psychic shop? Are you from Salem Village?"

"Did you say 'psychic shop'?"

"Yes. I had one in Salem Village for a few years, but then some lunatic came along and burned it to the ground while I was inside."

Oh my god, I thought. *It's her! I was right!*

"That was a while ago, though. Now Jared's taking me to Albany. Hopefully I'll find a job there. Maybe I'll open another psychic office."

Wait a second... What if I was right? What if this is a trap? So far, today has been one coincidence after another. First, I find a bottle with Boney's lover's address in it... Then, I magically find a train taking me to that address... And now, I find the woman who was somewhat responsible for my father's imprisonment... What's going on here?

Now hesitant, I responded, "Oh, wow. I'm sorry about your shop being burned—"

"It's nothing!" Sabrina exclaimed with a friendly tone. "I wasn't getting much business there anyway."

I have to be cautious, I thought. *I could have made a mistake by coming on this train... I was too focused on getting as far away from Greensburg as possible. Either I'm really lucky and paranoid, or I'm just really gullible.*

My line of thought broke when Jared asked, "What about you?"

"Pardon?" I replied.

"What are you going to do when you get to Albany? What's the nature of your trip?"

I couldn't trust either of them now, so I told them that I was looking for a woman named "Rose," the Rose who was in Boney's letter. By now, I assumed that the letter was fake, so I played into Mrs. Jamison's trickery and pretended that I was actually looking for "Rose".

I took out the letter with Boney's portrait on the back and gave it to Sabrina.

I started to say, "I'm trying to find…"

Sabrina cut me off once again.

"Rose," she said. "You want to find Rose!"

"How did you know who I was looking for?"

Sabrina replied. "Because the address on this letter is my grandmother's address, and my grandmother's name is Rose."

That's it, I thought. *This is a trap! I knew it! Mrs. Jamison probably created this whole charade to reel me into the train, and I was gullible enough to fall for her bait… Perhaps there's still a way I can get out of this. For now, I'll play along. I'll make these actors think Mrs. Jamison's trap is working on me, and slowly but surely, I'll find the right moment and escape.*

"Oh, and that's my grandfather's name!" She continued. "Sylvester!"

"He's your *grandfather?*"

"Yes, he is, but he died about six years ago. How did you manage to find that note?"

Boney's still alive. Mrs. Jamison is just trying to scare me. She's mocking me…

"Sylvester gave it to me himself," I lied.

Sabrina gave me a confused look and replied, "What? You knew my grandfather?"

"Yes. I was friends with him for a long time. He gave that letter to me in Salem Village during a court case. I was on the jury at the time," I said.

"Wow! What a coincidence!"

I replied, "I know, right?" in a stern voice.

She giggled and looked out the window. "What a small world."

35

Once we got to Albany, I marveled at all the buildings and cars that structured the city. It was all so noisy and dense, but vibrant at the same time. When the train came to a complete stop, I looked at my watch and noticed the train had arrived at noon. The sun was right above me and the streets of Albany were full.

I heard Jared and Sabrina talking beside me, but for a split second, they ended their conversation to say their goodbyes.

Jared said, "Well son, hope you enjoy Albany. It's really nice here in the morning, especially when the sun's out."

I shook his hand and hugged Sabrina, which was the traditional thing to do in this sort of situation, I assumed.

"I hope you enjoy meeting my grandmother," Sabrina added. "In a few days, maybe we can all get together and have lunch or something."

"Sure," I said. "That sounds wonderful…"

Jared and Sabrina took a step back and so did I. Eventually, I waved at them and turned around as we slowly drifted apart. I was now on my own, ready for Mrs. Jamison's trap to unfold if there was one to begin with.

Am I really being paranoid here? There was no way for Mrs. Jamison to predict where I was going. And there's no way that she could have made that love letter within a day and planted it by the lake with me constantly moving round…

If anything, this has to be real. Perhaps the person on this love letter isn't Boney and the people on the train were talking about

somebody else who coincidentally looks like Boney… At least, I hope
so.

Many of the streetlights were turned off and so were the lights in
the apartments. Some people were still waking up, getting ready for
another long day of work. Since I didn't want to waste my time, I
immediately brought out Boney's letter and looked at Rose's address,
realizing that I had no idea where I was in the process. I wasn't even
sure what street I was on. I needed help, so I looked around and
eventually noticed a newspaper stand resting directly in the center of
the city. The man inside leaned against the back of the kiosk as I made
my way over. I stopped and looked at him, hoping he would lead me to
Rose, or at least give me some sort of directions.

He was wearing a dark black shirt and slid his finger against the
board of the kiosk where people paid for their newspapers.

"Hello," I said.

The man looked up at me with a stern face. He mumbled, "You
gonna buy a paper or just stand there?"

I slammed Boney's letter onto the table and asked, "Can you
point me in the direction of this address?"

The man looked me in the eyes and frowned. He shook his head
and said, "I'll give you directions but you gotta buy a paper."

"Sure."

I looked into my jacket pocket and pulled out a small diamond.
As I took the stone out of my pocket and placed it onto the counter, the
man somehow immediately recognized that it was real and grinned.
Suddenly, he was the nicest person in the world.

He exclaimed, "So, what kind of directions do you need?"

As we talked, he was fiddling with the gem. He seemed to be ignoring me altogether.

I pointed to Rose's address and replied, "I need to find this address."

The kiosk manager still didn't look up at me. That diamond had put him into a trance as he tilted and shifted it around in a bunch of continuous circles.

Finally, he looked up at me and muttered, "Yeah, I know where this is."

"Really?"

The man smirked and pointed to an alley between two distant buildings.

"Go down that alleyway and take a right. It'll be the first red building you see on that street."

"Thanks."

"No problem."

The dark alley looked damp and gloomy. I entered it and a couple of kids were leaning against the walls, drinking something from an old paper bag. As I diverted my attention away from them, I noticed something odd about the alleyway; there was no right. There was only an old gray wall at the end of it. I realized that I had been lied to.

Wait... Was I right? I thought. *There's no way that this could actually be a trap...*

Am I really being paranoid?

Once I turned around, a group of people suddenly came together and closed me in. As I backed away from them, I said, "What do you want?"

The kiosk manager walked through the crowd. He looked at me as he rolled the diamond I'd given him earlier around in his left hand.

"You're stupid," he said. "You're a real fool."

"Leave me alone!" I replied, trying to push past everyone.

Nobody would let me pass. Around ten or twenty people were in the crowd. Most of them were silent while a few were whispering to themselves.

"Come on, you know what to do," the man said.

I was bewildered. "What do you mean?"

The entire group started to laugh.

"Hand us the rest of the diamonds you've got in that coat of yours," one of the men demanded.

"You heard him," The kiosk manager added. "Give them up. All of them."

In a harsh voice, I replied, "Go to hell."

He brought out a knife and yelled, "Give me that jacket you're wearing, or I'll cut you!"

I already noticed a couple of the thieves reaching for their guns, so I started to worry.

"You heard me!" He continued. "Give us that coat of yours before I take this knife and cut you with it! What are you waiting for?"

I was panicking. *What should I do? Do I fight back? Do I give them the diamonds and give up my dignity? Dammit! What do I do!*

Another thug from the crowd yelled, "Come on! Hurry it up already!"

Then the alley went silent; nobody seemed to move. I put my hands inside my jacket to reach for the diamonds.

"What are you doing inside that jacket? Take your hands of yours out of your pockets! Right now!" the kiosk manager demanded.

"Okay, okay!" I said, putting my hands into the air.

Suddenly, the kiosk manager smeared some sort of make-up from his face and laughed with the rest of the crowd, revealing Mr. Gliss's face.

I can't believe it, I thought. *I wasn't being paranoid! I was right! Why am I so stupid? I should've trusted my gut and ran!*

"Am I a good actor or what?" Mr. Gliss asked.

"How'd... How'd you find me?"

Mr. Gliss took a step closer. "When you escaped into those woods, I bribed a couple of rangers to spread this phony letter I wrote about Boney. I got his real name from some girl. Sabrina, I think. I told her that if she sees you, she should try her best to lead you here. But since there were so many places you could've gone, I decided to hire twenty or so fake Sabrinas to look for you on top of that."

I can't believe I was right all along... I played right into Mrs. Jamison's hands.

"And now you're here!" He cheered. "And I won't die! Mrs. Jamison will let me live! She'll let me live!"

I wanted to run but Mr. Gliss' men would have grabbed me. There was nothing I could do.

"And as for your friends—"

I cut him off, "What about them? What are they?"

"Dead..." he spat. "They're dead. Mrs. Jamison told me yesterday that she got a couple of her guards to go out and kill them. They tracked down Boney and his daughter and that Griff guys you're friends with and killed them all."

You're lying! I thought. *You're just trying to scare me. I won't listen to your lies! I know they're alive!*

I paused for a while and then continued, "And what about me?"

Mr. Gliss looked into my eyes. I froze in place as he took a rifle from one of the other men.

"We don't want you escaping again, Charles. I'd hate to kill you, but what else can I do?"

"Don't do this, Mr. Gliss. You don't have to do this…"

He got closer and pointed the gun at my head.

"Goodnight, Charles. Rest well, you deserve it."

Suddenly, I pulled a shard of glass from my jacket, as I'd always kept one on me. Without another moment to think, I jumped at Mr. Gliss and stabbed him with the shard. That was when I heard a loud *boom* erupt from his shotgun.

We walked into the darkness together.

I've been stuck talking about this calamity ever since my death. At the end of it all, I never got a grave, not in a proper cemetery. Instead, Mrs. Jamison spent a couple of dollars on her favorite bottle of wine which she buried next to the railroad, as per Frederick's request from prison. I never even got a funeral.

Maybe why I can never leave Greensburg… No one will let me. I get that I was killed in Albany. Some people say that they always remain in the spot where they died, but I ended up in Greensburg. Maybe I'm here because I resent this place so much, and that strong and hateful energy is keeping me around. I honestly can't explain why I'm here, but I am.

Now whenever I tell a story to the other ghosts, we all gather around a small patch of roses next to the train tracks and we talk about our pasts during the night. Just like tonight.